Fun with
Dick and James

Cat & Mouse Press

Cat & Mouse Press
Lewes, Delaware 19958
www.catandmousepress.com

This is a work of fiction. Names, characters, businesses, places, events, and incidents are either the products of the author's imagination or used in a fictitious manner. Any resemblance to actual persons, living or dead, or actual events is purely coincidental.

"Cocktail Croquet" appeared in an earlier form in *The Beach House*, published by Cat & Mouse Press, 2013.

"A Most Unusual Sweet Potato Competition" appeared in an earlier form in *Saints and Sinners 2016 New Fiction from the Festival*, published by Bold Stroke Books, Inc., 2016.

Copy editing by Joyce Mochrie
Cover illustrations by Mick Williams
Drink illustrations by Louisa Marcq
Cover Illustrations Copyright © 2016 by Michael Williams
Drink Illustrations Copyright © 2016 by Louisa Marcq
First printing, 2016
ISBN: 978-0-9968052-2-3
Printed in the United States of America

Cat & Mouse Press
Lewes, DE 19958
www.catandmousepress.com

Fun with
Dick and James

Rich Barnett

A Playful Publisher

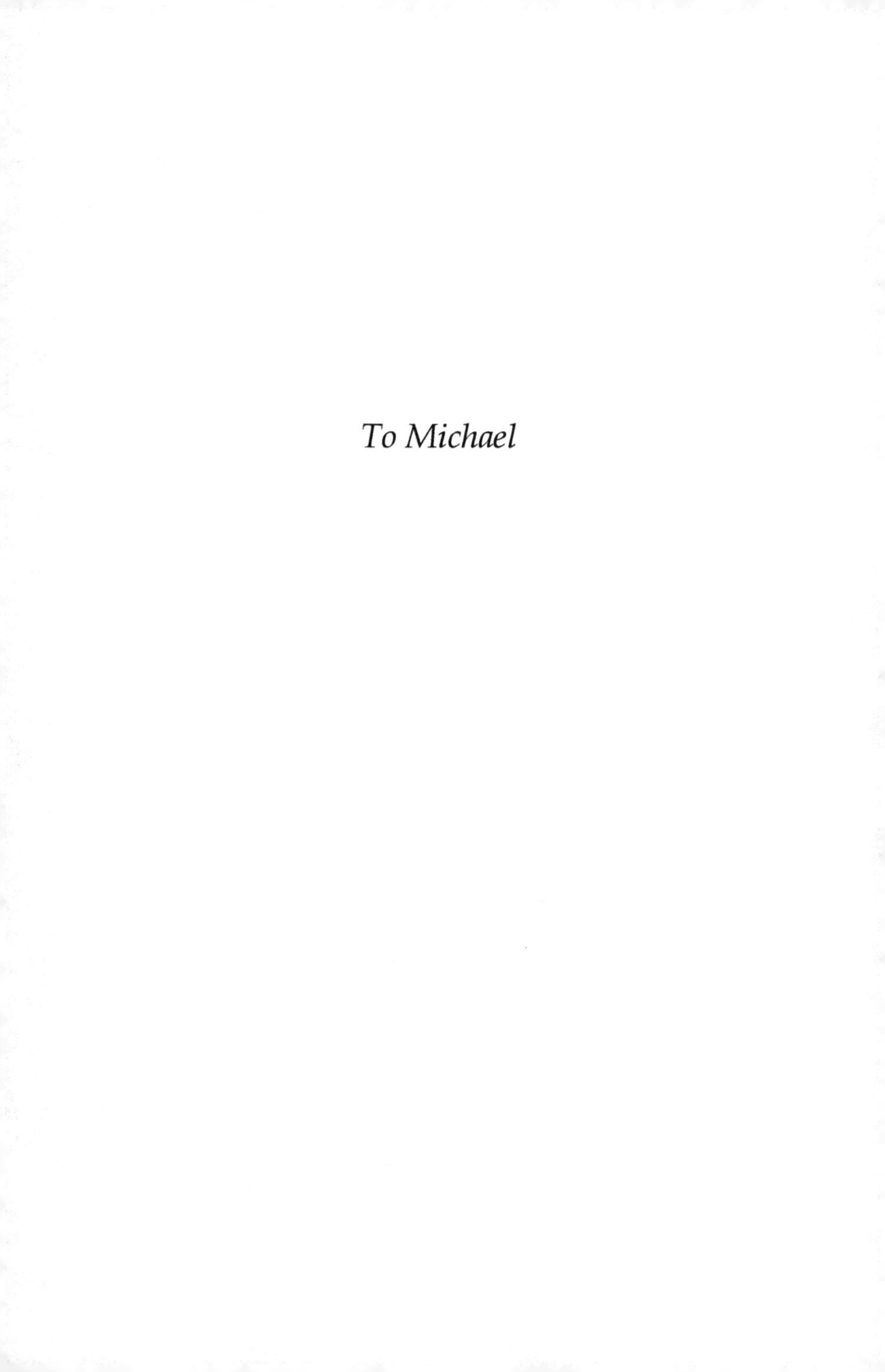

To Michael

Contents

Acknowledgments

For someone used to writing nonfiction for deadlines and within word counts, the freedom that comes with writing fiction is quite exhilarating. I can fib. I can let my imagination run wild. On the other hand, there's a reason people say truth is stranger than fiction, because fiction must also make sense.

I want to acknowledge a few people who have helped me navigate this new world of fiction writing. To Michael Craig: thank you for encouraging me always to be more grandiose. To Maggie Powell: thank you for making sure I don't stray too far over the edge.

I also want to give a shout out to my friends at Camp Rehoboth who for ten years now have provided me with a wonderful platform from which to develop my voice.

Last, but certainly not least, I offer BIG THANKS to my friend and publisher, Nancy Sakaduski, who approached me about this project and convinced me I was the right man to write it. I've learned a lot about the art of writing fiction from you these past twelve months. It's truly been a fun ride, and I look forward to more fun with you in the future. Cheers!

Cast of Characters

Dick Hunter

Tall, handsome (in a mature, Brooks Brothers sort of way), and old-money wealthy, Dick is in his early 60s. He came out of the closet late in life and moved into his family's "cottage" in Rehoboth Beach, where he is surrounded by his colorful friends, his ex-wife Kissy, and a basset hound named Otis. A few years ago, his life changed when he met James Flores. The difference in their ages and social strata raised an eyebrow or two (especially among Dick's family members), but Dick and James are now happily navigating life together. And although Dick would be perfectly happy to spend his days writing obscure historical biographies, taking naps, and lying on the beach, he seems to find himself in one jam after another.

James Flores

James is Dick's hunky Latino boyfriend. A former minor league baseball player, now fitness trainer, James is in his early 30s. He is not a gold digger, as some of Dick's family suspect; he just happens to be attracted to "silver foxes," a fact he attributes to growing up under the tutelage of older baseball coaches. James is an affable, natural problem-solver, which comes in handy each time Dick gets himself into yet another jam. The son of Mexican farm workers who became farm owners, James was born and raised in rural Delaware. He was the first in his family to attend college, and is very proud of his "American story."

Kathryn "Kissy" Hunter

Dick's ex-wife, Kissy, kept the Hunter surname when the couple divorced. It was an amicable split; Kissy often said she and Dick were better friends than lovers. Kissy and Dick met as young adults at a rainy point-to-point horse race when Kissy pushed Dick's sister Jane into the mud after being the target of some disparaging remarks. She's now a successful Rehoboth Beach real estate agent at the top of her game, and she isn't shy about slinging bling or going after what she wants. A redhead originally from Virginia, she's known for her fashion sense, flair for drama, fondness for Manhattans, and air kisses.

Fritz Wilmerding

A small man in his early 60s, with piercing blue eyes and an unfortunate henna rinse, Fritz Wilmerding is the scion of a failing, local french fry empire. With money running out, he clings romantically and desperately to the trappings of his former life — one that is literally and physically falling down around him. Fritz is Dick's best and oldest friend; they met as students in the library of the University of Virginia and were secret boyfriends for a while. Although he might have the attention span of a fruit fly, and some might think him a pest, nobody would ever consider him boring. Fritz is witty, a Francophile, and, in short, the life of any party.

Jane Hunter Stoutbury

Dick's older sister Jane is a bitter, pill-popping, prejudiced boozehound, and those are her good qualities. Her blue blood husband, Nathaniel "Big Nat" Stoutbury, currently resides in a minimum-security prison in West Virginia for embezzling. When Big Nat went to the big house, Jane fled her life in the chateau country outside Wilmington, Delaware, and is now hiding out in Henlopen Acres, the tony town nextdoor to Rehoboth Beach. Jane doesn't feel James is good enough for her brother. That, and Dick's homosexuality, cause tension in their sibling relationship.

Chip and Ashley Holzstock

Chip and Ashley are an attractive, young, blonde couple from the suburbs of Washington, DC. New to Rehoboth, they are trying very hard to assimilate, but tend to be a bit clueless. Chip is a successful architect with some family money, so the pair could afford to buy—and renovate—a home near Dick and James's. They like the idea of being part of the "cool" gay community but have somewhat of a tin ear, so their attempts to fit in sometimes are laughably off-key, but they mean well.

Rodney "Red Snapper" Snapp

Rodney Snapp is a society dentist from Wilmington whose family has been taking care of the smiles of Delaware's upper crust since the Civil War. He is wealthy, but homely and ill-tempered. With his thick lips, ruddy complexion, and bald head, he resembles a grouper more than a snapper, but the nickname bestowed upon him in boarding school is still used by his detractors. Red Snapper and Dick Hunter have been feuding for decades, but in recent years, Red has become obsessed with trying to make Dick's life miserable.

Fun with Dick and James

To Name or Not to Name?

*Dick's friends pester him to bestow a grand
name upon his "humble" cottage.*

"DO WE HAVE ANY SMOOTH PEANUT
BUTTER?" Dick yells out the open French doors of
the kitchen to his boyfriend, James, who is doing
calisthenics on the screened porch. "I can only find
crunchy."

"No smooth," the grunted reply comes back.

"How does he know without even looking,"
whispers Kissy, who is sitting beside Dick at his
round, oak kitchen table.

"Because James knows where everything is in
this house," Dick whispers back. "It isn't only his
body that's amazing."

"Need me to go get some?" James calls out.

"No, thanks; we'll muddle through."

Kissy lays her bejeweled hand on top of Dick's

and pats it three times. "*Muddle through*? Sugar, that is precisely the reason our marriage failed."

Dick extracts his hand from his ex-wife's. "No, dearest. It failed because I finally mustered the courage to come out of the closet."

"Don't go getting your panties in a wad." Kissy smiles sweetly at him and then slathers a glob of crunchy peanut butter on a toasted English muffin. "Promise to tell me if any peanut gets caught between my teeth? I have an appointment after breakfast."

Dick watches his ex-wife cut the English muffin into bite-sized pieces. He has to admit, Kissy is looking, as always, smashing for a woman who spends so much time in the sun and never strays far from a chilled Manhattan—up, of course. Speaking of which, he was certain some of her junkets to Manhattan weren't only for the fashion.

Whiskey, it should be known, is the spirit that brought young Dick Hunter and Kissy Fallwell together so many years ago at a rainy, point-to-point tailgate party. All the girls were huddled under a tent as if a little water might melt their pedigrees. Not Kissy. Rain be damned. She was slugging bourbon whiskey from a monogrammed silver flask and illegally betting on the horses. When she pushed Dick's older sister Jane into the mud for making disparaging comments about the fact that Kissy's family manufactured and sold enema devices, he'd been immediately smitten with the big, boisterous redhead from Virginia.

Their courtship had been quick. Kissy was under family pressure to wed, and Dick was certain he could marry himself out of his longings for men. The union had lasted a good thirty years, mainly because Kissy had been more interested in shopping and drinking than sex and babies. That Dick's family was one of Delaware's oldest and most prestigious didn't hurt, either.

When he finally confessed his homosexuality, Kissy had taken it in stride. At least he wasn't leaving her for another woman, she reasoned, and in the end, they had a good laugh.

The fact of the matter was that Dick and Kissy had always been better friends than lovers. After an amicable divorce, they decided to relocate to Rehoboth Beach, a place that seemed to hold promise for both of them. Dick bought out his sister Jane and moved into the family's summer cottage. Kissy started selling real estate and was now one of Rehoboth's top agents. She kept the Hunter surname and a top-floor, oceanfront condo in the town's most elite complex.

"Kissy, when do you plan to tell me why you really barged in here this morning? I know it wasn't for an English muffin."

She puts down her fork and slides her hands down the lapels of her yellow, tweed-knit St. John blazer. "Dick, I've decided you need my help if you are serious about reviving the Hunter family Daffodil Strut, and I won't take no for an answer. This town so needs a splendid party to celebrate the coming of spring."

"But …"

"No buts." She places her hand over his mouth until Dick finally nods his assent.

"You remember how upset we all were when your mother cancelled the Strut after your father died. She was convinced he loved his daffodils more than her. And I think she might have been right."

Dick pries off her hand. "I had to beg her not to have all the bulbs dug up."

"And thank goodness you did. Now, back to business. The first thing we must do," Kissy's tone turns serious, "is provide this cottage with a proper name. It would look impressive on the invitation, and first impressions are so important. You have to think about the details. This isn't the time to *muddle through*." Kissy stabs the remaining slice of English muffin with a knife and pops it into her mouth as James enters the room.

"How's the young athlete this morning?" Kissy eyes up the Latin man, who is wearing loose-fitting, gray sweatpants and a tight, white, sleeveless compression shirt. She used to wonder how it came to be that such a sexy young stallion — with his sculpted chest and milk-chocolate brown eyes — could be interested in Dick Hunter. Oh sure, Dick was trim and handsome in a Brooks Brothers catalogue, silver fox kind of way, but he was so much older than James. It had taken Kissy a while to realize just how fond James Flores was of Dick. Now she couldn't imagine either without the other.

"Just finished three hundred sit-ups." James leans down and gives Kissy a friendly peck on the cheek.

"I don't believe I could do ten." She pats James's flat belly. Dick rolls his eyes.

"People don't want their fitness trainer to have a fat waist. Wouldn't be good for business."

"See, Dick darling," Kissy exclaims. "James knows all about marketing."

James looks at Dick quizzically.

"Kissy is trying to convince me to give the cottage a name as a marketing ploy for the Daffodil Strut."

"It's an absolute must," Kissy says.

James grabs a sponge from the kitchen sink, wets it, and then goes over to Kissy. "May I? You have a bit of peanut butter on your jacket."

Kissy starts, as if finding a spider on her lapel, then relaxes as James dabs at the spot, deftly removing the offending peanut butter without leaving a stain.

"James, you are just so handy." Kissy smiles admiringly at James.

"I'll pick up a jar of smooth peanut butter later today," Dick says.

"You are a dear. Mwah! Mwah!" Kissy air-kisses, then grabs onto James's bicep, giving it a squeeze and using it as a crutch to help herself stand.

"Boys, I must be off. I'm showing the old Reynolds place to a darling young couple from Washington. He's an architect with big plans. Dick, dearest, think about a name. Tata!" she yodels on her way out.

"You've opened a can of worms this time," James says, and can't help but grin at his boyfriend.

"I know. But I'll need her help if I'm really going to bring back the Daffodil Strut."

"It's that big a deal?"

Dick nods, remembering the months of preparation his parents endured each spring to ensure one of *the* events of the year for the Social Register types of the Chateau Country and Brandywine Valley went off with style and seemingly effortless grace. Hundreds came to preen, drink, and strut about in their best spring attire, all the while admiring the Hunter family's award-winning daffodil garden. No expense was spared, from the champagne to the entertainment; pianist and cabaret singer, Bobby Short, from the Carlyle Café in New York was a regular. It was heaven for a young, closeted, gay boy like Dick.

"Tell me I don't actually have to strut," says James.

"It's the guests who strut."

"That's a relief."

"Trust me; it will be quite the undertaking."

After James pledges his support to help the effort and heads off to the gym and his morning training appointments, Dick pours himself a cup of coffee and pads off to his study, where his basset hound, Otis, is sleeping, oblivious to the morning racket. The study is Dick's favorite room in the cottage, a private, quiet space dedicated to thinking, reading, and writing. He'd even loved it as a young boy.

AFTER A LEISURELY HOUR SPENT WORKING on his latest writing project, a biography of Henry Cogswell, a millionaire crusader in the Prohibition movement who funded the building of temperance water fountains across the country, Dick feels a cold, wet nose press against his shin. Otis is awake and asking for his morning constitutional.

"Ready to go out, eh, old boy? OK, let's go check on the daffodils."

They stroll through the garden like an old married couple, Dick walking ahead and then slowing down to allow the hound to catch up. He had gotten Otis after his divorce because he had been so lonely rambling around the big, cedar-shake cottage by himself. The dog had developed some joint and back problems and was prone to flatulence, but he was a good companion. And his nose was in perfect working order. Otis could spend hours sniffing about the garden, if Dick would only permit.

The Hunter family home had been built by Dick's grandparents on a very large piece of property in the Pines neighborhood on the north side of Rehoboth Beach in 1929 before the Great Crash. The property backed up to Lake Gerar, one of the three, small, freshwater lakes in the town. Grandfather Hunter had wisely paid to dredge and clean up the lake in exchange for nearby land, which he then developed for the old-money set from Wilmington and Washington who spent their summers in Rehoboth.

Gardening had been Grandfather Hunter's diversion from work, both in Rehoboth and at the family homestead outside Wilmington. Dick recalled hearing stories about the tough steel industrialist's annual battles with Bunny Smith, a feisty dowager gardener, for daffodil supremacy at the Philadelphia Flower Show.

Dick's father had inherited not only the family galvanized steel wire and paper clip manufacturing business, but also its green thumb. His father continued the daffodil plantings and initiated the Daffodil Strut as an annual fête. Dick and his sister Jane used to sneak drinks and cigarettes while the grown-ups weren't paying attention. The gardens were where Dick felt both the burden and the comfort of his family. Naturally, he felt it was his duty to carry on the legacy.

His daffodil reminiscences are interrupted by the loud voice of Fritz Wilmerding, longtime friend and secret boyfriend during their years at the University of Virginia. A short, handsome man with piercing blue eyes and an unfortunate henna hair rinse, Fritz lived nearby in the old Wilmerding family home, surrounded by rare books and expensive antiques, despite the fact the house was practically falling down around him.

The Wilmerdings had been bootleggers during Prohibition before turning respectable, using their ill-gotten gains to buy up real estate and start a local chain of now iconic, but failing, french fry concessions. Fritz had, in fact, been named after *pomme frites*. For years, he ran the Wilmerding Gallery in downtown Rehoboth until the afternoon a couple came in looking for a painting of seagulls. Fritz hurled a glass paperweight at them, and the police had to be called. It seemed he was no longer able to deal with the tourist trade, and that was that. Now, he existed on a rapidly decreasing inheritance and the occasional sale of furniture, silver, and art.

"Ah, here you are. I was ringing the doorbell and knocking and yelling." When Fritz reaches down to give the hound a playful scratch on the head, Otis passes gas.

"Sorry about that," says Dick. "Otis and I are checking on the progress of the daffodils. Look at this — the tête-à-têtes are about to bloom. The Dutch masters won't be far behind. In a month, the entire place will be in bloom. Not a lot of time to prepare for the Daffodil Strut. There is much to be done." Dick reaches down and removes a stray leaf from the walkway.

"Indeed! That's just what I've come to speak to you about. I ran into Kissy. Here's a book I want you to take a look at. It's called *The Last Resorts* by Cleveland Amory. Amory writes about the noble tradition of naming one's cottage."

"Not you, too." Dick eyes the old, green hardback, spotted with black mildew, an ever-prevalent problem along the coast, particularly in the region of the Wilmerding dining room. Dick notices that Fritz's loafers have the same spots.

"It was fashionable in classic resort towns like Newport, Bar Harbor, and Palm Beach for grand owners to give grand names to their grand homes. The Breakers, Pointe d'Acadie, Mar-a-Lago — they evoke such a picture of the stately life. I can't believe your family never named this cottage." Fritz is waving the book in Dick's face.

"Perhaps they felt it too pretentious for Rehoboth?" Dick ventures.

"Ah, but not every grand dame and grand monsieur played by the rules. Amory also writes about how Newport society was aghast when one Tennessee family named their home Chateau Nooga. One *can* be playful."

"Or not."

"Well, Kissy and I are one hundred percent certain. In fact, I've been noodling it around and have come up with the perfect name. Want to hear it?"

"I'm not sure."

"*Narcissy.*" Fritz extends his arm toward Dick in a grandiose gesture as the name rolls off his tongue with exaggerated s-sounds.

"Excuse me?"

"Narcissy. It pays homage to its owner—that would be you—as well as to the thousands of narcissi planted in the garden. Did you know that 'daffodil' is an old British term for a gay man? It's pure camp perfection."

"Well … it's that … but it's just, uh, it's just too *gay.*"

"Puhleeze. We have gay marriage." Fritz snaps his fingers loudly. "And everyone knows you're a practicing homosexual. You've got to get over the self-loathing. It's not an attractive trait."

"I am not self-loathing."

"Hmm. Well, that's to be determined."

"You're no psychologist."

"That's true, although I have noticed—"

"OK, OK," says Dick. "I suppose the right sobriquet

would create an impression—of what, I'm not certain."

"That's the spirit! Now, I've got to run. James will be annoyed with me if I'm late for our work-out again." Fritz delivers a bicep-flex pose. "Today, we're working on guns."

"I thought you were against firearms."

LATER THAT DAY, Dick is in the kitchen mixing up a batch of French 75 cocktails when James weighs in on the house naming.

"I can't believe how aggressively Fritz was pushing this house naming thing on me during our training session at the gym. Don't you find it a tad silly?"

Mwah! James is interrupted by the sound of an air-kiss emanating from Dick's phone.

"It's a text from Kissy. I have no idea how she gets them to sound like that."

"She must have downloaded a ringtone," James says with a smile.

"Well, you know I don't know about those things, and I can't imagine why anyone would care."

These were the times when Dick realized that he and James were more than just a few years apart. They had met at Azul, a popular gay watering hole, where James was working as a cocktail waiter after a knee injury ended his minor-league baseball career. He was the summer's hot new number, and his athletic physique fanned the flames of desire among Rehoboth Beach's sizeable gay community. Dick was astonished, but delighted, to have captured the heart of the handsome, young Latino, even though they came from such different backgrounds. James was more farm and field than horse and hound, but somehow it all worked out.

Dick looks at his phone. "She's got an idea for a house name."

Mwah!

"Boite Bois," Dick reads from the iPhone.

"Bwhat?"

"It's French for 'wooden box' and slang for a nightclub. She and Fritz ginned it up, pun intended. Well, no doubt about it, they nailed it. We have wood shingle siding and a wood shingle roof. There's wood paneling throughout. And we *do* like our nightly cocktails. What do you think, James?"

"Do you even want to name this place?"

"I've warmed to the idea, and I do think it'll be good for promoting the Daffodil Strut. Kissy and Fritz have put so much thought into this, I don't … I just can't decide."

"You know, you don't have to choose one of their ideas. You can come up with your own name."

Dick pauses and tilts his head. "Why, you're absolutely right!"

"In my opinion," James begins, "the name should be one worthy of respect."

Dick nods in agreement. "The Hunter family has always been a pillar in Rehoboth. This cottage is classic, not at all like the modern monstrosities popping up all over town. I'd venture so far as to call it dignified. We have a formal living room, a proper dining room, and the kitchen is out of sight. None of this open living concept hogwash."

"Right. Why would you want people watching you peel carrots or scrub pots, or whatever else you might want to do in a kitchen?"

Dick sniffs the air and looks around, his eyes landing on Otis, who is lying quietly by the French doors. "A name shouldn't be too fussy. I mean, really — we do have an old, farting basset hound here at Hunter House."

"That's it!" James is grinning.

"'Too Fussy'?"

"No."

"'The Farting Hound'?"

"No! What you said: 'Hunter House.'"

"*Hunter House*. I do like the ring of that. Do you think Fritz and Kissy will be disappointed if I don't use one of their names? They put a lot of thought into this, much more than I have. Will they forgive me?"

"Of course they will. They always do."

"Speaking of forgiveness," Dick says, "I just remembered that I was supposed to buy some creamy peanut butter. I want to avoid a repeat of this morning's fiasco if Kissy drops by again for breakfast."

"Not to worry. I picked up a jar on my way back from the gym."

"Thank you." Dick leans over and gives James a kiss. They clink their glasses and toast the naming of Hunter House. "We'll celebrate tonight because starting tomorrow, we've got a lot of work to do."

"I suppose you're right."

"After all this fuss, if I don't make the Daffodil Strut a success, you'll be looking for a boite bois to bury me in."

In the end, Dick needn't have worried. More than a hundred people attended the renewal of the Daffodil Strut. Guests took the theme to heart and were fashionably and playfully attired in all shades of yellow. Most women—and some of the men—sported decorative hats. James pinned a daffodil on everyone upon arrival. The highlight of the party, everyone agreed, was when the genteel host led guests through the daffodil plantings in an informal, conga-line parade while playing the kazoo. Some of Dick's upstate friends who came south for the event said it was the best Strut they could remember, which made Dick feel enormously proud.

Had the house really needed a name? Dick didn't think so. But the more he thought about it, the more he liked it. *Hunter House*: the name felt solid, authentic, and emblematic of the no-drama life among family and friends to which he aspired.

Pennies from Heaven

Dick receives an unexpected windfall.
What to do with all that money?

THERE WAS SOMETHING STRANGE ABOUT THE LETTER from Greene Brothers. Dick passes the high-cotton-count envelope from hand to hand, as if looking for someone to pass it along to. It had arrived two days after the receipt of his quarterly dividends statement, so it was clearly not a regular notice. And Greene Brothers wasn't known for superficial client communications. That's why the firm was so popular with those who still clung to the notion that conversations about money are vulgar.

He gingerly slices open the creamy white envelope with a sterling silver letter opener engraved with the initials JRH, the same as his father and grandfather. It's a succinct letter and, just as he thought, it contains some unusual news. His recently deceased Aunt Evelyn has left him a half-million dollars and a 1959 Nash Metropolitan convertible. A snapshot of the car slides out of the envelope.

Dick sits down in his favorite wing chair in his study. This certainly was an unexpected development. The money had already been deposited into his everyday account. And the car, according to the letter, would be delivered in just a few days.

Mwah! Mwah! Mwah! Dick didn't need to look at his phone. The air-kiss ringtone set to the tune of an electronica disco beat announced a call from his ex-wife Kissy, who ironically never got along with Aunt Evelyn.

"You're never going to believe this," he begins, and goes on to explain the content of the letter.

"Then my timing is perfect. I think you should put that windfall toward an investment property in Dewey Beach," Kissy replies, before Dick can even finish telling the story.

Dick is flabbergasted by the suggestion. Dewey Beach, the small town just south of Rehoboth, is known for its noisy bars and rowdy tourists.

"Dewey Beach is honky-tonk."

"It's undervalued. Everyone is looking to get in. I know a place."

Twenty minutes later, they're standing at the front door of a squat, white cinderblock house. A half-dozen plastic Adirondack chairs and an empty beer keg grace the sand-and-crabgrass front yard.

"Anyone home?" Kissy calls, and loudly taps on the door with a key before entering the living room, which is littered with pizza boxes and red plastic cups. A young man lies splayed out in his under-wear beneath a beer-pong table.

They approach the man. "Is he dead?" Dick asks.

Kissy squats down and gently puts the back of her well-manicured hand under the man's nose. "No, he's breathing. Just passed-out drunk, I suppose." She runs her hand lightly over his muscular chest.

"This place is a dump." Dick looks around, taking it all in. "It'll cost much too much to fix up."

"You're not going to renovate it, darling," she says with a laugh. "You're going to trick it up. Despite what you think, this house has a great rental history."

"Somebody would rent this?"

"It's mere steps to the beach. My guess is these boys are bartenders and lifeguards. They don't care about décor; they just need a place to lay their pretty heads." She strokes the cheek of the sleeping young man.

"Why don't *you* buy it then?"

"Because I don't have a spare half-million dollars from a dead auntie burning a hole in my pocket." Kissy stands. "Here's what you do. Rent it out for a few years, and then tear it down and build a nice, new house with a pool that I can sell for a big profit. I'm recommending property in Dewey Beach to all my clients now that the Rehoboth city commissioners have started passing such extreme building regulations."

"They're not extreme. They're designed to keep out McMansions."

"Says the man who already has his mansion. I'm telling you, Dick, real estate in Dewey is gonna pop."

"But I don't want to be responsible for renters — no matter how attractive they are." Dick eyes the still passed-out young man. "How can they drink so much and still have such perfect stomachs?"

"I wish I knew."

"I'd be a terrible landlord. You know I'm uncomfortable talking about money with strangers."

A FEW DAYS LATER, THE NASH METROPOLI-TAN arrives at Dick's cottage on Pine Cone Lane.

"I love the black-and-white houndstooth upholstery." Dick reaches in and brushes the seats of the classic car.

"So who was Aunt Evelyn again?" James is fondling the car's gear stick.

"She was mother's younger sister," Dick says, slapping James's hand away.

Evelyn was the longest-living of the Butler beauties, the three daughters of the president of the University of Pennsylvania. They were known for their looks and charm, and later, for marrying extraordinarily well. Evelyn married a Getty oil heir and lived a somewhat secluded life in the hills of Laguna Beach, south of Los Angeles. She drank vodka, supported the local arts scene, and curated a spectacular cactus and succulent garden.

"And *you* were her closest relative?"

"Aunt Evelyn never had children. She always invited me along on her grand cactus-hunting excursions throughout the Southwest and Mexico. They made those fancy African safaris you hear about look bourgeois."

"Why'd she leave you the car?"

"Perhaps because I enjoyed driving it when I went to stay with her after my divorce. Aunt Evelyn was extraordinarily understanding when I came out of the closet, much more so than my immediate family. She assured me that every family worth its salt has a homosexual."

Dick smiled, remembering how she'd escorted him to Laguna's infamous Boom Boom Room, where they spent many nights sipping martinis and watching the sun set over the Pacific. She even tried to fix him up with a has-been movie idol friend of hers.

"She was never fond of Kissy, but she *really* disliked my sister Jane."

"Wonder what she left Jane."

"A particularly prickly cactus, if I know Evelyn."

"It says here that your aunt purchased the car from a dealer on Hollywood Boulevard. It cost $1,799." James is reading from the documents that accompanied the car. "It's in excellent shape. The papers say it's been garaged since 1998."

"It will make a splendid beach buggy."

"We can't drive this car on the beach."

"You don't think so? It's very lightweight."

"It will be perfect for driving *to* the beach. Our chairs and umbrella will fit in the back seat. We'll make quite a picture."

"What a beauty!" Fritz calls, as he pedals up to the car on his bicycle. "All it needs is a low-digit license plate."

Fritz, like many old-school Delawareans, has a fetish for low-number, black-and-white license plates. It began when the state started issuing license plates. Wealthy people who could afford to buy those early cars received the first low-digit license plate numbers simply because they were issued in numeric order. A status symbol was born. Delaware allows license numbers to be transferred and passed down through generations. The result, many say, is that low numbers are more desirable than a Rolls Royce or a Tesla. Fritz's Volvo station wagon may be dented and scratched and covered in stickers, but a closer look will reveal a black, three-digit plate.

"Many Delawareans count a low-digit license

plate in his or her estate planning. It holds its value better than gold or silver," Dick says to James.

Fritz grimaces. "You make it sound so Republican. A regular buff-and-blue license plate would disgrace this extraordinary car, and you know it. Listen—Buck Everest is having an auction next week. I hear there's a low-digit tag on the list."

"I don't know. They're so showy. James, what do you think?"

"I can't believe I'm agreeing with Fritz, but yes, I think a special car from a special aunt deserves a special tag. You should at least go see what's up for bid."

"LOOK AT THE SIZE OF THIS CROWD," Dick says, as he and James take their seats on the far end of a row a little more than halfway toward the back of the auction room. Fritz had arrived early to save what he claimed were the best seats from which to bid. One wanted to be close enough to the auctioneer that he could quickly see your paddle, but far enough away to be removed from the sight of most of the other attendees. Per Fritz's instructions, they had dressed conservatively. Serious players understood the importance of discretion.

Buck's auctions are always well-attended, but this one has drawn what looks to Dick like about four hundred people. He notices that, in addition to the low-digit license plate, the auction also includes artwork and furnishings from the home of a flamboyant and recently deceased Rehoboth Beach restaurateur.

"Quelle chance!" Fritz gasps, and clutches his throat as the auction begins with a box of the restaurateur's shoes.

"Who'd want his old shoes?" James asks, wrinkling his nose.

"Child, you don't understand," Fritz explains. "Most of them are from Bergdorf's."

Fritz pats James's arm and raises his paddle at the starting bid of $400. "I've always coveted her crocodile bow moccasins. They don't even make them anymore." He raises his paddle at $500, then at $600. "Of course, they'll be a little big, but I'll just stuff some newspaper in the toes."

"I have $600 on the floor. Do I hear $700?"

A young man raises his paddle. Fritz grips James's arm.

"Do I have $800? Who will give me $800? I have $700 going once, going twice—"

Fritz waves his paddle right before Buck slams down the gavel.

"We have $800 now, ladies and gentlemen, $800. Will anyone go $850? For $850, you can slip into the swankest shoes in all of Rehoboth."

The auctioneer leans down, nose in the box of shoes, and inhales dramatically. "Smells like money!" he announces. The crowd laughs, breaking the tension. "I have $800—$800 going once, $800 going twice. C'mon folks, loosen the rubber bands on those wallets."

"I can't look," Fritz moans, burying his face into James's shoulder.

"Sold!"

Fritz bolts out of his seat in exuberance and takes a bow to the applause of the crowd. James looks at Dick, who just rolls his eyes. As if Fritz needed any more fancy shoes.

"Look, look," Fritz squeals. "Her custom-made bed is coming up next. I hear the chintz headboard still has pomade stains! Oh, if that bed could tell tales—"

The bed and the rest of the furnishings sell for much less than expected, with the exception of the artwork. Buck Everest, however, can sense the crowd's restlessness and knows it is time to change direction.

"Ladies and gentlemen, next up we have the pièce de résistance, the item you're waiting for." All talking ceases.

"This particular two-digit license plate has never been on the market. Do I hear $50,000?"

Bidding quickly reaches $100,000, and then passes $150,000. The audience is cheering and chanting "go for it" to spur on their favorite bidders. Buck Everest knows he has a hungry crowd, so he pauses and holds up the plate.

"Ladies and gentlemen, all numbers are not created equal. This particular two-digit number belonged to the late Lowell Small, a world traveler and a collector of fine and decorative arts made in Delaware and Pennsylvania. It has been missing for decades. Until now."

Buck has the crowd in the palm of his hand. They are hanging on his every word. He pauses for a moment and then nearly whispers: "Who will give me $200,000?"

Dick raises his paddle. "My father was friends with Lowell," he says to James.

"Ladies and gentlemen, there is one among us, one brave heart, one man bold enough to put $200,000 on the table." The crowd erupts in cheers like nothing Buck Everest has seen in all his years of leading auctions.

"But I have to ask—will anyone do 210? Two hundred and ten for a once-in-a-lifetime opportunity." All heads are turning, looking around to see if any of the early bidders will continue to pursue the plate.

Pressing on, Buck continues: "Just a few months ago, this plate was discovered by a museum intern in the drawer of a Greek-revival-style desk that was in rather poor condition and thus relegated to an off-site storage facility. The museum, as custodian of Lowell Small's property, is putting it on the market. The funds raised will support a new exhibit about the Greek revival movement in Delaware and, in particular, Delawarean sympathies for Napoleon during the early nineteenth century." He gives the crowd a knowing look before continuing with the bidding.

"Two hundred and ten going once," he calls. "Going twice." A paddle is raised in the back and quickly lowered. "Two hundred and ten to the new bidder in the back!" The audience responds with claps and cheers.

"Game on," Buck yells. The crowd loves the drama. Dick, James, and Fritz, on the other hand, are stunned by the last-minute bid and crane their necks, looking toward the back of the room to see who has jumped in.

Buck strings out the friendly back-and-forth competition with small incremental increases until the bidding hits $250,000.

"Ladies and gentlemen," he announces with great gravitas, "we are approaching a milestone. Seldom do low-digit license plates go for more than a quarter-million dollars at auction. But then we seldom have such storied license plates as this one. Like Starbuck and Ahab's great white whale, we knew it was out there somewhere." He holds up the plate and then, to the surprise of everyone in the convention center auditorium, walks down the middle of the aisle between the seats showing off the black-and-white license plate.

"We have two bidders still in pursuit," Buck explains. "I have but one plate. The question is simple, the answer is complex. Who wants it more? Who has the courage to cross the line and give me 260?" The crowd is hushed.

"$260,000!" yells Buck, pointing to the back of the room. "Do I have 270?" Even before he finishes asking for the bid, Dick raises his paddle.

While the audience is clearly enjoying the drama, James senses something is amiss. Just who is this bidder in the back, coming in so late? He must have passed muster to bid, but still—

James quietly slips out of his seat and walks to the back of the room, where he spots the bidder in dark glasses and a baseball cap. James watches the bidding rise to $300,000, at which point the mystery bidder takes off his hat to wipe his forehead. James frowns, recognizing the bald man despite the sunglasses. It's Red Snapper, Dick's nemesis.

Rodney Snapp, known as Red Snapper by those who dislike him, is a society dentist from Wilmington whose family had been taking care of the smiles of the state's upper crust since the Civil War. He'd picked up his unflattering nickname in boarding school, given his ruddy complexion and unfortunate resemblance to a fish.

Though Rodney Snapp and Dick Hunter had grown up in the same social circles, they'd never been friends. At the tony St. Andrew's School, Dick had beaten out Rodney for a place on the varsity tennis team. In later years, Dick blackballed Rodney's petition to join the Society of the Cincinnati by calling attention to his faulty historical genealogy. Dick said it wasn't personal, but Rodney believed otherwise. More recently, Rodney had pursued James mercilessly and had never gotten over James's rejection. His jealously toward Dick Hunter for winning the boy's affections had only grown and become more toxic.

As a result, he delighted in spreading malicious gossip and lies about Dick. Last year, Red Snapper had purchased a cottage on Pine Cone Lane, and the two settled into what everyone in town thought of as a quiet, but competitive, détente. But behind the scenes, Rodney continued to seize any opportunity to undermine Dick.

James knows what he has to do. He quickly retakes his seat and whispers to Dick.

On the auction stage, Buck Everest plays his final card.

"Ladies and gentlemen, I have just been informed that a writer for the venerable 'Grey Lady' has entered the room. Although, we should not be surprised that such a historic occasion and the sale of such an important piece of Delawareana has attracted such attention."

What? The *New York Times* in Rehoboth? The buzz

in the room reaches high-summer cicada level.

Raising his hands to quiet the crowd, Buck calmly asks for a bid of $310,000. Dick waves his paddle immediately, as he has throughout the auction.

"I really want this license plate," Dick states in a loud voice.

Fritz shushes him, but it is too late; the word is out. If Dick had been looking to the back of the room, he would have been blinded by Red Snapper's megawatt smile.

"Will you give me $320,000?" Buck asks, pointing to the bidder at the rear of the convention center. When the paddle goes up, a woman in the crowd screams.

"I guess it's 3–2–5, 3–2–5, and that's no jive! Who in the room will go 3–2–5?"

Buck waits. The crowd waits. Heads turn to see Dick Hunter sitting patiently, paddle against his thigh. Buck, too, looks at Dick, awaiting some sign. But Dick sits immobile as a statue.

"We have 320 going once, 320 going twice." The audience is silent, as if no one wants to break the spell. "Speak now or forever hold your peace."

The gavel slams onto the wooden podium. "Sold to the gentleman in the back for $320,000!"

There's a sharp gasp from the rear of the room, and the crowd erupts in cheers.

Departing the auction, Dick and James can't help but smile when they overhear Red Snapper pleading with Buck Everest to get out of the bid, all the while trying to put off the *New York Times* reporter. Fritz lets loose with a loud chuckle, which prompts a corresponding hiss from Red Snapper. What the trio didn't hear was Red Snapper's muttered pledge for revenge.

TWO DAYS LATER, DICK HUNTER WRITES A CHECK for $15,000 to Buck Everest Auctions for a four-digit, black-and-white license plate.

"Once we realized Red Snapper was the other bidder," Dick tells Kissy, who has dropped by for a glass of champagne and to christen the car, "we knew he had no real intent to purchase the plate. The fiend was just driving up the price on me."

"But how did you get out of the bid?" Kissy asks.

"It was all James's doing. He knew the Snapper couldn't resist bidding if he knew I really wanted the plate, and once he took the bait, all I had to do was stay quiet and let him win."

"So how did you get this plate, then?"

"James heard some additional plates would be coming to auction and figured we could get one for a good price, since the Snapper wouldn't dare try that trick again."

"Clever boy."

"Yes, he is. I think this number is better anyway," says Dick. "Ironically, it's the same year the car was manufactured. I'm sure Aunt Evelyn would be pleased."

"You sure are lucky that James has *your* number," says Kissy.

"And my back."

"So true," Kissy says, as she looks wistfully over at James, who has finished attaching the plate to the car.

A Good Chair is Hard to Find

Dick and James get skunked.

"MON DIEU! YOU WEREN'T KIDDING. This place reeks of skunk." Fritz Wilmerding fans the air with a slow and exaggerated gesture. "Where is the old stinker?" Fritz looks around for Dick's basset hound, Otis.

"He's in the study. Won't budge out of my reading chair."

"How long has he been in there?"

"At least an hour."

"An hour!" Fritz drops his arms and gives Dick a cutting glance. "Girl, you've got to get that hound off that chair or you'll be living with the eau de skunk forever!"

"He won't come when I call. Perhaps he's embarrassed?"

"Where's James?"

"He's at the doctor."

"Oh dear. Nothing disabling—or disfiguring—I hope. Now, where was I? Oh yes, your skunked hound. Dick Hunter, sometimes you are such a sissy."

With that declaration, Fritz sashays down the hallway from the kitchen to the study, where he finds Otis with his head buried between the seat cushion and the back of the wing chair. Dick follows, reluctantly.

"How on earth did this happen?"

"I let him out for his morning constitutional," Dick explains, "and the next thing I know, he's yelping and charging into the house, faster than I've seen him move in years. He ran straight to my study and leapt onto that chair. He hasn't moved since."

"Fritz grabs the old basset hound around the stomach and lifts him up and out of the chair, which causes Otis to start farting. "C'mon, Old Faithful, you're going into the tub." Fritz hauls the gassy hound into the bathroom just off Dick's study and hoists the dog into the claw-foot tub.

"Be a dear, Dick, and fetch me the blue bag I dropped off in the kitchen." Fritz has the faucet running and is wetting Otis down when Dick returns.

"Inside. Hand me that bottle."

"Bloody mary mix?"

"I didn't have any tomato juice, so I'm improvising."

"Why do you need tomato juice?"

"Don't be silly. It's the only way to get rid of

skunk smell. Everyone knows that." Fritz empties the bottle over the dog and begins to rub it in. "This isn't going to be enough. Do you have any more?"

"I'll check." Dick returns five minutes later with a large jar of marinara sauce.

"You're kidding?"

"It's all we've got." Dick hands Fritz the jar. "It's made from tomatoes."

Fritz pours the sauce over the hound and kneads the mixture into Otis's fur. Operation Odorless Otis is going well until Fritz raises the dog to wash his belly at exactly the same moment that James arrives home. At the sound of the front door opening, Otis, perhaps sensing an opportunity to escape his tomato torment, wiggles out of Fritz's hands. The hound slithers out of the tub and scrambles into the study, stopping every now and then to shake, which launches sprays of marinara sauce and bloody mary mix several feet in every direction. Before Dick and Fritz can grab him, Otis has made it back onto the wing chair.

Hearing the yells and yelps, James enters the study to find Dick and Fritz trying to lift the wet and howling hound out of a tomato-splattered wing chair.

"What the hell is going on? It looks like a crime scene in here, and you two look like the victims. What's that smell?"

"Don't ask," Dick replies.

A FEW WEEKS LATER, OVER BREAKFAST WITH KISSY, Dick is relating the story and explaining the difficulties he's had in finding a replacement for his no-longer-favorite reading chair, which is now emblazoned with pink blotches and still giving off a skunky odor, despite having been treated twice with a steam cleaner.

"I don't mind the faint aroma of skunk," Kissy muses, "especially on a beautiful fall night when I'm driving with the top down in the beamer."

"You mean 'bimmer.' 'Beamer' refers to a BMW motorcycle, and 'bimmer' refers to a BMW car."

Kissy is spreading smooth peanut butter on a couple of English muffins. "This is why we're no longer married. You're always correcting me."

"Only when you're mistaken, my dear."

"Seriously, Dick," Kissy changes the subject. "How hard can it be to buy a chair?"

"You've no idea. It has to be comfortable and stylish, but not too."

"Sort of like a Gucci loafer, I suppose."

"Exactly."

James, smirking at the repartee between the two, brings out a fresh plate of English muffins, along with ramekins of smooth peanut butter and jelly.

"Darling, what's this?" Kissy holds up a ramekin filled with amber-colored jelly.

"It's guava."

"What's guava?"

"A tropical fruit about the size of an apple. It's sweet and fleshy, and used to make candies and jellies. My mother always gave us peanut butter and guava sandwiches. It's a Latin thing."

"Oh, really? I like Latin things." Kissy gives James a long look and then slathers smooth peanut butter on an English muffin and tops it with a spoonful of the golden, guava jelly. She bites in. "My heavens, this is divine! Where can I get some?"

"I buy it from one of the Latino grocery stores out in the county. I'll pick up a jar for you if you'd like."

"Aren't you sweet. Mwah! Mwah!" She delivers a few air-kisses and turns back to Dick's dilemma. "You were saying ... about the chair. . . ."

"I looked all over Rehoboth. I saw some lovely chairs, of course, but everything seemed to have a beach motif. Seashells, palm trees, and cabana stripes are not my style."

"Too *Golden Girl*?"

"I scoured Washington, too, but nothing was quite right." Dick sighs. "Mitchell Gold had some "unique and ethical pieces" that would have been fine if I were purchasing a sculpture. Room and Board's were too mid-century modern. And besides, who can wait four to six weeks for delivery from some vegan furniture artist in Wisconsin?"

"Have you tried the catalogues, darling?"

"Everything seems too deep. I want to sit in a chair, not lie down in it. Anything I did like seemed to be available only in taupe. I'm at the end of my taupe rope."

"What color is taupe, anyway?" asks James.

"A gray brown, I believe." Kissy pulls out her phone and does a quick search. "Apparently, it's French, a derivative from their word for the common mole. Sometimes it includes a touch of lavender." Kissy looks at Dick. "You cannot select a color named for a mole. Especially a common one."

"Ahem." James clears his throat and sits down at the table with Dick and Kissy. "I have an idea. I'll be finished with my last client by three. Pick me up, and we can drive out to Selbyville to look for chairs."

"*Selbyville?*" Kissy gasps, clutching her pearl necklace. "You can't be serious. I went there once to look at a potential real estate listing. The roads are riddled with signs about bed bugs and Jesus. What kind of chair can you find there?"

"Believe it or not, it is a bit of a furniture hub and has been for a long time. Trust me." James gives Dick a reassuring shoulder squeeze. "What have you got to lose?"

"Nothing, other than a smelly chair."

James pats Dick's back. "OK, then its settled. Pick me up at three. I'm going to walk to the gym."

AT PRECISELY THREE O'CLOCK POST MERI-DIEM, DICK DRIVES UP in the black-and-white Nash Metropolitan convertible.

James stares in disbelief. "Um, why are you driving the smallest vehicle we own for a trip to buy furniture?"

"I'm not worried," Dick says with a yawn, "because I'm certain we won't find anything appropriate. And if we do, we'll have it delivered."

James reluctantly gets into the car, casting a skeptical glance into the tiny back seat.

The men stop first at Johnny Johnson's, the largest furniture store on the East Coast. "Good Lord," Dick exclaims as they park the car, "it's the size of an airplane hangar."

They enter the 190,000-square-foot facility and pick up a map that shows the locations of the various furniture showrooms. It is, Dick feels, eerily reminiscent of being in a Las Vegas casino where one quickly loses all sense of time and place.

They stop at a room that seems to contain thousands of chairs of all different styles and sizes. There might even be a few that happen to be suitable, but

Dick can't focus on finding them. He stares, mesmerized by all the people rocking back and forth in humongous ultra-suede recliners and spinning to and fro in upholstered swivel chairs, as if trapped in some sort of human pinball machine.

Dick and James walk over to an unoccupied white leather recliner. It has a large tag on it that explains its features, which apparently include a retractable chip-and-dip holder.

James climbs into the enormous chair and reclines it fully, striking a pose. "Look, it even has a space for the remote. You've got to try this." James gets up and motions to Dick.

Against his better judgment, Dick climbs into the recliner. "I've never been on one of these," he tells James, sprawling backward. "I admit it's comfortable, but it's not very sophisticated, is it? I can't imagine watching *Masterpiece Theatre* like this."

Dick and James are so engrossed with the recliner that they fail to notice a man watching them from the adjoining showroom. Nor do they see him snapping photos of Dick Hunter trying out the white recliner.

"How embarrassing for Dick," Red Snapper says quietly to himself, as he uploads the image to Facebook. He had spotted the distinctive black-and-white Metropolitan while on his way to the Department of Motor Vehicles nearby and followed it to the store. Now he had been rewarded for his efforts.

Dick gets out of the recliner. "We need to go. I'm over-stimulated, and not in a good way."

BY THE TIME THE MEN ARRIVE at Crenshaw's Furniture, Dick is still delirious from the furniture vortex he's just escaped and has to walk around the car a few times just to clear his head. When Dick and James finally enter the establishment, a short, fleshy gentleman in a bright-red, wool waistcoat rushes up to greet them.

"Welcome, welcome," he says, flushed with excitement. Dick looks behind himself to see who this dandy is so thrilled to see.

"Yes, I'm speaking to you. Welcome to Crenshaw's. How may I serve you?"

Repressing the urge to laugh, Dick explains how he is looking for the right chair for a proper gentleman's study, but on coming off a rather unsettling experience at Johnny Johnson's, he's prepared to give up.

The fleshy man licks his lips, as if preparing to give a speech. "Well, gentlemen, you've come to the right place. Permit me to introduce myself. I am Preston Crenshaw." He adjusts his tie delicately.

"Do I detect an English accent?" Dick asks.

"No, I was born here in Selbyville. I did, however, study interior design at Drexel, and then across the pond at the University of Buckingham. England is where the Crenshaws originally came from and where I met my wife, Jemima."

"Your wife!" James blurts out, giving the effeminate man a look up and down.

"Jemima!" Dick adds.

"Oh, I can tell you two are naughty boys." He wags his finger at them. "Follow me. I have a few chairs you might like. Some special pieces for special clients."

He takes James's arm and leads the men on a winding path through the store. "Crenshaw's," he says, drawing himself up to his full height, "is one of the oldest family-owned businesses in Delaware. We used to furnish all of the more refined families in lower Delaware. Senator Townsend was a big client. Look, here's a photo of the senator with Eleanor Roosevelt. He was as staunch a Republican as she was a Democrat, yet here they are. It was chicken that brought them together."

"Chicken?" James asks.

"The Senator raised them, and Eleanor wanted to raise them. They put politics aside to talk chicken. It was a delicacy back then. Of course, you know the modern broiler industry started not far from here. And besides, who doesn't like chicken." He runs his hand down James's back before pulling a purple velvet drape aside to reveal a showroom the likes of which Dick and James have never seen.

A row of majesty palms graces a tall, southern-facing glass wall. There are stacks of furniture everywhere, in the middle of which sits an enormous, purple velvet sofa. It looked to be about the same size as the Nash Metropolitan. Miniature paintings and gold-framed mirrors cover the grass cloth walls. There's even a white cockatoo. To call it a sun porch or a Florida room would be unkind. This was a furniture folly.

Dick and James watch as Preston feeds the bird a few sunflower seeds.

"Lovely Lucille, lovely Lucille," he says in falsetto.

Preston shows them a few chairs, beginning with a chartreuse, leather barrel chair. "I love this domed, burlap wing chair, too," Preston says. "I imported the fabric from Austria."

James glances at Dick.

"Now this pair of Louis XVI Bergères en Cabriolet date to the last quarter of the eighteenth century. They're from the Kennedy family home in Virginia. I snapped them up at the big Kennedy auction at Sotheby's in 2005. Paid just a smidgeon over twenty thousand dollars, but oh, so worth the price, don't you think?"

"Absolutely," Dick replies. "May I?"

"By all means." Preston giggles as Dick eases his

lanky frame into one of the antique chairs.

"Not too comfortable."

"Of course not."

"What are those?" James points to a couple of flowered chairs, peeking out beneath a red blanket.

"Ah, the young man's eye isn't merely pretty," Preston replies, lifting off the blanket with a flourish to reveal two classic club chairs. "I personally think these chairs are divine. I love the bold, but masculine, floral pattern. A small family company in North Carolina makes them. Quality craftsmanship with a little southern flair. Please try them out. I'll be right back."

Dick and James sit in the chairs, which they agree are perfect, and, most importantly, do not swivel.

Preston returns with a silver tray upon which sit a bottle and three tiny, tulip-shaped glasses containing an amber liquid. "Thought we might take a late-afternoon sherry. This is a lovely amontillado, which is a little nutty. As the clock approaches dinnertime, I find sherry creates a hunger, a sense of anticipation."

"A *little* nutty?" James murmurs under his breath.

Dick stands. "Mr. Crenshaw, we —"

"Please, call me Preston."

"All right, Preston. How soon can we have these two chairs delivered?"

"Week after next, perhaps? My delivery man is

away in Atlantic City on his honeymoon."

Dick shoots James a look James knows all too well.

"Our car is not very practical," James admits, "but I am. If you can rustle up some bungee cords and rope, I'm sure I can figure out how to truss 'em up and tie 'em down for our drive back to Rehoboth Beach."

"Oh, I'm sure you can." Preston giggles and refills James's glass.

"I earned a Boy Scout merit badge in knot-tying."

"Of course you did."

After a couple glasses of sherry, James carries the chairs out and arranges them on the back seat and trunk of the Nash Metropolitan. Preston takes Dick's credit card and returns with a roll of jute rope.

James slides the rope underneath the car and then up and around the chairs. Preston is attempting to help, but Dick notices he is doing more touching than tying.

"Hey, look at this." James points out to Preston that the white price tags attached to the chair with safety pins contain different prices.

"Oh dear. Let me check." Dick and James follow Preston back to the register, where the receipt for the chairs is still on the sales desk. It indicates a sale at the higher price of the two tags.

"Oh, my. Someone must have marked them

down without telling me. Well, in any case, you gents are getting a real deal." He hands them the sales receipt.

"Are you going to re-run that card at the lower price?" James asks, increasing the pressure of his squeeze of Preston's shoulder.

"Oh, silly me. Must be the sherry. Let's take care of that." Preston re-runs the card and hands Dick a new receipt for the lower price.

"I can always count on James to sort out a co-nundrum." Dick is beaming; Preston is not.

As they drive back to Rehoboth with the precious cargo, Dick can't help but wonder why it is that chairs seem so much more difficult to pick out and purchase than other pieces of furniture. It's about more than comfort, he thinks. Is it because they're more like us than are beds and tables? Chairs have arms, legs, and backs. They can be staid, frumpy, or trendy. He looks over at James, who is gazing contentedly at the passing landscape. Perhaps, he thinks, it's that they also support us when we need it.

Cocktail Croquet

*Will the gentlemen's game remain
a gentlemen's game?*

"HOW ABOUT WE ROUND UP THE USUAL SUSPECTS for cocktail croquet this afternoon?" Dick suggests to James, who is hunched over his laptop. Dick walks over and tousles James's hair.

Although the focus tended to be more on cocktails than croquet, the game had become a tradition in Rehoboth, with games scheduled on the fly, weather permitting and when the spirit moved the hosts.

"That'd be fun. If you set up the course, I'll handle the food and booze. Kissy can help us with the invitations. And according to the Weather Channel," James pauses as he pulls up the website, "we can expect sunshine and a light breeze blowing in from the ocean later today."

Mwah! Mwah! Mwah!

"I swear that woman is clairvoyant," Dick says with a laugh, reaching for his phone.

"Kissy, we were just talking about you. By chance are you available for cocktail croquet this afternoon? Yes, you'll be teamed with Fritz again. And you'll help with the invitations? The usual suspects. And we'll need a fourth team. No, I hadn't thought about Chip and Ashley. Yes, they are lovely, and I know they're new in town, but you know *you* are our token straight." He holds the phone away from his ear before finally getting in the last word. "OK, OK. Invite them if you must."

Later that afternoon, while arranging the shrimp tower and placing tea sandwiches on the outside bar, James asks Kissy and Fritz for their opinions about his light-blue, oxford shorts embroidered with red roses.

"They're a little snug," he says, tugging at the waistband.

"Bootylicious!" says Kissy, reaching over to give James a playful slap on the rump.

"How do you even know that word?" Fritz asks. He eyes James's backside. "A little more than snug. In fact, if they weren't so preppy, I'd say they'd border on lewd."

"Should I change?"

"Definitely not," Kissy and Fritz exclaim in unison.

"We could use some eye candy around here," Kissy adds, taking in Fritz in his baggy, faded, kelly-green pants.

At precisely six o'clock, competitors and spectators begin to arrive on foot, by bicycle, and in cars. Soft Cole Porter tunes waft from the house. Lil and Helen, a couple who live on a boat in Lewes Harbor, show up with their Portuguese water dog, Capitano. All three are wearing blue-and-white captain hats. A group of Fritz's friends have come to root him on. They arrive carrying a cheese platter, pulling a little red wagon filled with ice and bottles of bourbon, and brandishing silver pompoms. They were "traveling well," to use a college football phrase.

Behind the parade come Ashley and Chip Holzstock, tall, blonde, and nattily attired, all in white. Chip is wielding his own croquet mallet.

"Oh dear," Fritz and Kissy gasp, hands simultaneously reaching toward their necks in matching clutch-the-pearls gestures. They stare unabashedly at the scene unfolding before their eyes. Ashley Holzstock is approaching with a large bottle of white wine in each hand.

Cocktail croquet is where expectations are turned upside down. It might look polite, but it can get downright cutthroat. Pomp and circumstance? Dismissed. Rules? The hosts interpret them. But liter bottles of pinot grigio? Absolutely not. As Dick Hunter often said, "This is cocktail croquet, not wine and wickets."

Kissy grabs Fritz's arm. "C'mon, let's skedaddle. I'm not getting involved."

"But they're *your* friends. By the way, I've been meaning to ask how that dreamy Chip got his money? Did he marry it?"

"I hear he's from an old Pittsburgh family. German."

"Well, I do declare, I'm coming down with the Teutonic Plague!" Fritz fans himself.

Kissy gives the Holzstocks a fluttery wave and quickly hustles Fritz away, leaving James to play host and deal with the faux pas in process.

"So glad you could make it." James greets Chip and Ashley. "I don't know where Kissy and Fritz took off to. Let me introduce you to Lil and Helen. They're clients of mine and regulars for croquet."

James witnesses Chip and Ashley's confusion as they look from one woman to the other. People always have a hard time telling the sporty couple apart, given their matching haircuts, expensive Scandinavian eyewear, and propensity for Lacoste shirts with the collars standing up.

"Pleased to meet you," Lil replies, giving the bottles of white wine the stink-eye.

"We are so excited. It's our very first cocktail croquet match," Ashley explains.

"So I see," Helen says.

At this point, James takes charge, grabbing the bottles from Ashley and ushering them over to a smaller bar, where he uncorks a bottle and pours wine into clear plastic tumblers emblazoned with the phrase "Cocktail Croquet" in a flamboyant script font.

"Hope you don't mind these instead of wine glasses," he says, handing them the tumblers. "It's our traditional cocktail croquet cup. Look, I'm putting the wine down here in the cooler to keep it cold. You'll be OK refilling your own, won't you? We never have a bartender anymore because everyone we know likes to make their own. A stronger pour, you know. And don't you both look spiffy in your matching white pants and white shirts."

Ashley heads off to find Kissy, and Chip follows James over to the east lawn, where Dick in his Nantucket red pants is kneeling on a copy of *New Yorker* magazine and pushing the last wicket into the ground. When he stands up, James hands Dick a French 75 cocktail in one of the ubiquitous tumblers.

"Unusual course set-up," Chip says. "It looks somewhat like a classic nine-wicket, two-stake, double-diamond arrangement, but you've made some unorthodox wicket placements."

Dick raises an eyebrow. Chip Holzstock appears to know his croquet. Rather than laying out the course in the flat middle section of the back lawn, Dick has arranged many of the wickets on the perimeter along slopes that lead directly into flower beds—where dozens of low-slung azaleas and rhododendrons lie in wait—and close to a couple of huge oak trees with ancient roots that will disrupt the run of the ball. Truth told, it was a difficult course.

GAME TIME. DICK EXPLAINS THE RULES and assigns each team a colored ball. "Hit your ball under a bush, and you must play it as it lies, no matter what contortion you are forced to undertake in order to do so. There are no out of bounds. It's all part of the course."

To determine who goes first—an advantage for an experienced player—each team takes a turn hitting its ball as close as it can to the big oak tree in the middle of the course. The crowd is surprised when Chip Holzstock wins the challenge, his black ball coming a couple of inches closer to the tree than Dick's blue ball.

Over the next hour, Chip and Dick battle it out like two heavyweight boxers. Dick, who has been playing croquet since he was a young boy and later won tournaments at the Merion Cricket Club, has home-field advantage and knows each rut and bump on the course. Chip, it turns out, has an incredibly deft touch with a mallet. Ashley, after a few glasses of white wine, lets it slip that Chip had been an Imperial Wicket at St. John's College in Annapolis during his senior year, when the team beat both Harvard and the Naval Academy.

Most of the crowd, on the other hand, is hanging out by the bar, laughing, drinking, and discussing dinner plans, team members taking their turns only when called. They aren't paying attention when one of Rehoboth's finest arrives on the scene. A neighbor, it seems, has complained about the noise.

"What noise?" Kissy asks the square-jawed, young policeman. "This is a well-behaved lawn party. May I mix you a Manhattan?"

"No, thank you. I'm on duty. Are you the owner of the property?"

"Heaven's no. My ex-husband is … um, officer, are you married?"

"No, ma'am."

"*Ma'am?* I am not a ma'am!"

"Ma'am, I'm looking for the owner."

Kissy glares at the policeman, trying to figure out how to upbraid him in a flirtatious way when Dick arrives.

"Officer, this is my home. Is there a problem?"

"One of your neighbors called to report a loud party."

"Are you serious?"

"Yes, sir."

"Does this look or sound like a wild party to you?" Dick extends his arm in a dramatic gesture.

The policeman looks around, taking in the empty liquor bottles, discarded pom-poms, and dog wearing a navy-and-white sea captain's hat. "Sir, I am obligated to respond to all complaints and to remind you that we have a noise ordinance in Rehoboth."

"Did that prissy old queen Red Snapper complain?" Fritz has stepped between the police officer and Dick. "It's just because he wasn't invited. You should arrest him for filing a crank report."

"Whack!" Dick jumps at the sound of Chip Holzstock sending the blue ball off through the shrubbery. The officer reaches for his gun. Kissy screams and spills her cocktail on her new, navy-blue, needlepoint slippers. Fritz falls to the ground and covers his head.

"Keep calm, folks. It's just a bonus shot, and a very good one at that," Dick explains, at which point everyone begins to laugh, including the policeman.

"Officer, are you sure you don't want to stay and play?" Kissy says, placing her spa-tended hand on the policeman's arm. "I think my partner's nerves are shot." She nods toward Fritz, who is spilling bourbon everywhere as tries to pour himself a drink.

"I appreciate the offer, ma. . . ." He catches himself. "I'm afraid I'm on duty until midnight." He tips his hat to Kissy and departs.

Back on the course, Chip is assisting James in hitting the blue ball out of a particularly thick patch of English ivy. Dick wanders over to observe. As James steps up to address the ball, Chip walks up and places his hands on James's waist.

60

"No, here," Chip says. "Let me show you the proper stance. You're not playing golf. Stand facing where you want the ball to go." Chip moves closer behind James and repositions his hips. "Spread your legs for me a bit."

Dick's jaw drops.

"That's right," Chip continues. "Now swing that mallet through your legs. See how good it feels. Take a few practice swings and get a sense of the power and control you have with that stroke. The trick to this particular shot is to chip at it and halt the stroke as soon as you strike the ball. You want it to jump."

"Thanks," James says. "I think I've got it." Chip's hands, however, remain glued to James's waist.

Dick looks over at Ashley, who seems oblivious to the manhandling her husband is giving young James.

Finally, James extracts himself from Chip's embrace. Whack! The noise captures everyone's attention as the blue ball sails up and out of the ivy. Smack! It hits the oak tree in the middle of the course and ricochets onto the bar, causing Fritz to drop to the grass again. Ring! The blue ball bounces into the empty, silver, shrimp serving bowl, picking up a coating of remoulade sauce before rolling off the table and back onto the course, where it ever so gently bumps up against Chip and Ashley's black ball, as tender as a mother-in-law's kiss.

It was a highly improbable, yet entirely legal, shot—for cocktail croquet, that is. Because the rules permit it, Dick takes the opportunity to send the black ball bouncing toward the perennial garden, where it rolls down a flagstone path toward the lake. James then taps the blue ball through the final wicket, striking the peg.

Wahoo wah! Wahoo wah! Dick blows his silver kazoo in victory. It had been a close match.

As the competitors freshen their drinks and kick back to enjoy the rest of the evening, Dick Hunter strolls to the edge of the lawn, where he stands, mallet in hand. He takes in the scent of fresh grass and notices the flicker of the first fireflies, which have begun to emerge, as if by magic. *This was a good day with good friends*, he thinks to himself.

James wanders over, taps his mallet against Dick's, and says: "To the victors."

Losing His Drag Cherry

*Dick agrees to participate in a charity
event. What could possibly go wrong?*

"FRESH PIES, FRESH PIES, COME AND GET 'EM," yells the seven-foot-tall "woman" in a blue, beehive wig and white tunic as she descends imperiously down the steps of a yellow trolley car being towed by a pickup truck, which just seconds before had screeched to a halt in front of Dick Hunter's cottage on Pine Cone Lane. "Marie Antoinette," "Jackie O," and "Madonna," all of whom are wearing beatific smiles and bearing apple pies, follow behind "Lady Liberty."

The final drag queen to exit the trolley is attired in a black, one-piece bathing suit, white high heels, and a red headscarf. The crowd in attendance — tipsy from bloody marys and mid-morning Manhattans — cheers as "Little Edie" proceeds to perform a dance number to the tune of the Virginia Military Institute fight song, while waving an American flag. What would Independence Day in Rehoboth Beach be, Dick wonders, without a visit from the

Pie Ladies, an ad hoc drag troupe who travel the town on this most patriotic day to deliver delicious pies and good cheer?

"Who's 'Little Edie'?" Ashley Holzstock asks Dick after the song-and-dance number comes to a close.

"An eccentric cousin of Jackie Onassis," Dick explains to the thirty-something neighbor as patiently as he is able. "Little Edie and her mother, 'Big Edie,' lived in squalor among cats and raccoons in a run-down mansion in East Hampton known as Grey Gardens. Oh, it was a scandal. They say Jackie had to send them money to pay their taxes. They drank rum and were known to eat cat food at times."

"No!"

"The Maysles brothers made a famous documentary about them. I've often wondered if someone one day will make a film like that about Fritz Wilmerding."

Ashley looks at him wide-eyed, but before Dick can explain to her about the gay cult that has arisen around Grey Gardens — or what he means about Fritz — Little Edie grabs him by the arm and proceeds to tell him all about the Prohibition Pageant, a special drag benefit the Pie Ladies are organizing at Azul, the popular Rehoboth watering hole, to help raise funds to renovate the Women's Temperance Union fountain on the boardwalk and get it on the state historical register.

"Why," Dick asks, "would the Pie Ladies be involved in such an effort?"

"Because the Pie Ladies like a cool drink of water." Little Edie waves her flag in Dick's face and goes on to explain how they're big supporters of the Rehoboth Museum and want to help. "Most people just walk by without recognizing this little monument to the grand, and thankfully failed, experiment of Prohibition."

"I'd love to help," Dick says. "By coincidence, I'm writing a book about Henry Cogswell. He spent his fortune building temperance fountains across the United States."

"Well, how 'bout that," Little Edie replies.

"I can certainly help with the application for the historical register. I've got lots of reference material and old photographs."

"That's fine and dandy, but will you be in the pageant?"

"Oh, I don't know about that. I've never done drag. Didn't get the gene. Research is more my style."

"Please, baby, please" Little Edie implores. "It'll be fun. The Pie Ladies will get you your own stylist. And it's for a great cause."

"Oh, you should," Ashley chimes in. "You have great legs."

"For a man of your age," Little Edie adds.

Dick looks at Ashley and Little Edie, not quite sure how to respond to their comments. Caught up in the spirit of the moment, however, Dick agrees to participate in the fundraiser.

Dick's acquiescence sends Little Edie off in glee, waving her flag and singing a temperance slogan: "Lips that touch liquor will never touch mine; Lips that touch liquor will never touch mine."

DICK STARES IN THE MIRROR. "Good Lord, she's right," he says to Kissy. "The teased-out purple wig looks more sophisticated than the cotton-candy pink one or the big, white bouffant."

"I couldn't agree more," she says, clapping her hands.

"And I can't believe I just used the words 'teased out' and 'bouffant' in the same sentence while referring to myself."

Dick and Kissy are sitting in the Little Shop of Wigs, a small store jam-packed with wigs of all shapes and sizes. Drag queens—and older straight women—from across the Delmarva Peninsula flock to the store for the unique product selection and to its owner, Mrs. Kim, for her expert guidance. Rumor has it she used to supply all the wigs for the big production numbers at the Trump Casino in Atlantic City back in the day.

The diminutive Korean shop owner approaches

them, carrying a wide-tooth comb. "See, I tell you color go well with your eye." She teases the hair on the wig a bit more and adjusts it to better fit Dick's head. "You trust Mrs. Kim." She holds out her hand. "Buy now?"

Dick and Kissy's next stop is Fabú, a dress store for plus-sized ladies located on Coastal Highway behind a liquor store.

"Oh, my," Kissy exclaims, after they enter the dark and very cold establishment. She'd never seen so many sequins—in so many colors—and in so many large sizes.

"The Pie Ladies highly recommended this place."

"I can see why."

Kissy waves off help from the matronly shopkeeper and drags Dick over to a rack of sixties-style dresses that look to be the best of the bunch.

"I'm thinking something Twiggy-inspired for you."

"Twiggy? Wasn't she super-thin?"

"Darling, don't be so literal. Her fashion sense was simple, with lots of straight lines."

Kissy quickly paws through the rack of dresses before stopping at a pink sequined number. "I just love, love, love a classic shift dress in a bold color." She pulls it out and holds it up to Dick. "It'll go splendidly with oversized eyelashes. And we won't even need to shave your chest."

"Shave my chest? I don't think … isn't it a bit, uh, racy?"

"For God's sake, Dick. You're going to be wearing a purple wig. Have a little fun."

Dick pondered that for a moment, trying to figure a way to salvage some modicum of dignity. "I was thinking something long and black, like this one here." Dick pulls an elegant sequined gown off the rack.

"Listen, sugar, trust me. You're going to be in a wig and makeup. You'll want something that stands out and creates a *look*. This little pink number will sparkle under the lights. Plus, it will coordinate perfectly with your white Gucci loafers, which solves the question of what you're going to wear on those big feet of yours. Scoot now; try it on."

"Try it on?" Dick says, his glance darting around the store.

"Darling, we have to see if it fits. Here, take the black gown, too."

Dick reluctantly takes both dresses and heads toward the dressing room at the back of the store.

"I'm not really a cross-dresser," he mentions to a few older women who are waiting their turn for the dressing room. They look at him blankly.

He tries on the black gown first and is surprised to find it actually fits quite well. He is just pulling the pink dress over his head when Kissy calls out to him.

"Come out so I can see you."

"Well, well," Kissy remarks when Dick emerg-es wearing the pink shift. "Not bad, not bad at all. We'll have the waist taken out a couple of inches—there's room here," she tugs on the dress. "It'll be perfect. Love the length. You know you still have great legs."

"So I've been told."

"C'mon now. Let's get it and then go to lunch. I desperately need a Manhattan and a chicken salad sandwich before my next showing."

They head to the cash register with both the pink and the black dresses in hand. Dick figured he would buy both and decide later which one to go with. James would know.

THE DRESSING ROOM BACKSTAGE at Azul is like a locker room before a football game. Dick looks around at men in various stages of undress, psyching themselves up for the pageant. Some are listening to music. Others are standing around, chatting with their fellow competitors. A few are tucking and taping.

"Dick Hunter? I'm looking for a Dick Hunter," yells a burly, young man with a shiny, shaved head.

"Me, too!" someone yells.

Even with that line, the intensity in the room is such that hardly anyone laughs.

"I'm Dick Hunter," Dick waves to the fellow, who directs him to a chair in front of a mirror a bit out of the way from the crowd. True to their promise, the Pie Ladies have lined Dick up with a make-up artist.

"I'm Ralph, and I'll be doing your hair and makeup." The two men shake hands. "Hey, I think I know you. Don't you date that studly Latino personal trainer?"

"I do."

"Lucky fella. So I understand you've never done drag?"

"Correct."

"Well, let's get you fixed up, then. Where's your wig?"

Dick pulls the purple wig from a shopping bag.

"Amazeballs," Ralph exclaims. "And what will you be wearing?"

"I haven't decided." Dick brings out the black gown and the pink sequined shift.

"Cool," Ralph declares, hoisting a large, silver, metal box up onto a table. He flips the catch and it opens, revealing several tiers of makeup.

"Tell me that isn't a tackle box," Dick says.

"OK, I won't. But we all use 'em," Ralph replies, as he begins to powder Dick's face. "Home Depot. Seventy-nine dollars. Virtually indestructible.

Besides, I need an especially big box for my bait." Ralph presses against Dick's arm as he begins to apply foundation.

Well, well. Dick is amused and a little flattered, but says nothing and does not press back. He'd heard some gay hairdressers use such a ploy to flirt with their customers, but he'd never experienced the practice firsthand until now.

Strangely, the experience of being made up isn't as unpleasant as Dick had imagined. He actually enjoys watching his transition through the big dressing room mirror. He is also amused by the fact that Ralph is listening to a NASCAR race on his phone while working.

"I'm a big fan," Ralph explains to Dick. "I grew up near the US 13 Speedway over in Delmar. I used to race dirt track. My first boyfriend worked in the pit crew for the Jeff Gordon Number 24 team. He was older. Sexy, but stupid."

Within an hour, Dick begins to see where this is going. He looks like a cross between Dame Edna and Paula Dean. All the while, Ralph is explaining everything he is putting on and also telling Dick how to remove everything afterwards. It doesn't sound too difficult.

After about ninety minutes of nonstop work, Ralph tells Dick it's time to put on the dress.

"Put on the pink one so we can see the color."

Dick wiggles his way into the pink dress.

Ralph steps back and rubs his chin. "Something's missing. A bright-colored lipstick would be too cliché. Wait, I know." Ralph disappears, leaving Dick sitting in the chair, admiring his new persona in the mirror and finding himself ridiculously pleased.

Have to give it to Ralph and the Pie Ladies, he thinks. *This is a top-notch job.*

Finally, Ralph returns. He is palming a big pair of cherry-red, ball earrings. He clips them onto Dick's earlobes. "Perfecto!"

Damned if Ralph isn't right, Dick thinks. And just like that, he's no longer Paula Dean, but instead Twiggy's hip, somewhat older, slightly heavier sister.

Ralph gives Dick a slap on the butt to wish him luck. "Told you I wouldn't be too rough on you for your first time. I'll be rooting for ya tonight."

Just then, a man in a blonde wig, wearing a red dress with a revealing split, approaches Dick. "I didn't know you were entering the contest," the stranger says to Dick. The blonde notices the blank look on Dick's face. He leans over and whispers, "It's me, Chip Holzstock."

"Good Lord, I didn't recognize you! You look so, uh, good."

"I know. Ashley dolled me up. She even insisted on shaving my legs for the bathing suit competition." Chip runs his hands down his muscular legs. "I've shaved before," Chip continues, the tone of his voice deepening. "Triathlon, you know. Heck, hair will grow back. And it's for a good cause."

"We have to wear bathing suits?"

"There's always a swimsuit competition in a beauty pageant. The entry form spelled it all out."

"What form? I never got a form."

"Well, there are three parts to tonight's pageant: evening gown, swimsuit, and talent."

"Talent? I don't have any talent. I thought I just had to appear on stage for a few minutes in a dress."

"Nope, it's the whole trifecta."

"What are you doing for talent?"

"I'm gonna twirl a baton."

Dick tries to formulate a response but can't come up with anything that seems appropriate.

"Ashley taught me. She was a majorette at Auburn. Hey, didn't you play in a college marching band?"

"Not a real instrument."

"Just the skin flute, eh?" Chip gives Dick a playful punch on the shoulder.

"Huh? No. It was the kazoo. Will you excuse me, please?" Panic is setting in as Dick quickly calls James.

"How's the prep going?" James asks, upon answering the phone. "I can't believe you're actually going through with this. I'm so proud of you."

"I need a bathing suit!"

"What?"

"I need a bathing suit. A woman's bathing suit.

And there's a talent competition, too. I need to do something so I don't look like a bloody idiot."

"Slow down," James says. "We'll work something out. Tell me what you need."

A half-hour later, James arrives backstage at Azul with a bag and a French 75 from the bar. "Here, sip this." He hands the libation to Dick, who gratefully takes a big gulp.

"Actually, you don't look as bad as I'd expected," James says with a laugh. "Kissy thinks this will fit you," he says calmly, as he pulls out a lime-green, Lilly Pulitzer, one-piece bathing suit with a skirt. "It's from the time when she was a more substantial gal. And Kissy insists you wear her add-a-bead necklace for good luck," he says, handing it to Dick.

Dick takes it reluctantly.

"Be gentle; you know how she loves it."

"You should wear the black dress for the evening gown competition and the pink shift for the talent. Here, I brought your silver kazoo. You could hum 'The Good Old Song,' or. . . ."

"Or what?" Dick asks, feeling calmer now that James is taking charge.

"If you really want to win—which I think you can—I have an idea."

James looks around and then pulls Dick into a quiet corner of the dressing room and explains. "I'll just need to return to Hunter House to gather up a few supplies."

THE EVENING GOWN AND SWIMSUIT COMPETITIONS had gone off without a hitch, and Dick is feeling he might have a shot at the crown. Backstage, he and the other contestants are watching Chip Holzstock finish twirling a baton to the tune of "Dixie."

To Dick's surprise, Chip dropped the baton only twice. The second drop, however, was a doozy, as the baton hit the stage on its rubber tip and then bounced crazily into the judges' box, striking the African-American drag queen, Chanel Sweetbooty, who had been none too pleased with the song selection to begin with.

"Imagine if the baton had been on fire," Ralph whispers into Dick's ear as he gives Dick a quick touch-up. "I heard he was considering it. And he says he's straight. . . ."

Dick's stomach does a flip when he hears the emcee announce him as the evening's final contestant. *One more to go.* He takes a deep breath and slowly glides onto the stage, looking resplendent in purple wig and pink sequined shift. He is pushing a white, wrought-iron, patio-style bar cart. The music starts up, and Dick begins singing, "You're Just Too Good to Be True," the Frankie Valli classic and one of the few songs he knows by heart.

The spotlight beams in on Dick as the audience begins swaying and singing along to the chorus of the song, which is always a crowd pleaser. On the bar cart is a gallon of Plymouth gin, a bottle of Veuve Clicquot, a silver flask, a bowl of lemon halves, a silver ice bucket with tongs, a cocktail shaker, a package of napkins, and five champagne flutes.

Continuing to sing, Dick masterfully pours gin into the cocktail shaker, squeezes the lemon halves to extract their juice, and carefully measures in the liquid from the flask. He gives the mixture several long, hard shakes in order to achieve a nice, frothy consistency, and then fills each glass. He pops the cork off the champagne bottle in a dramatic gesture and tops the drinks with bubbly.

Several audience members recognize the action and realize that the judges are about to experience Dick's signature French 75 cocktail. Applause and a few cheers break out.

Dick hands each judge a cocktail napkin and a filled glass. Judge Sweetbooty stands to accept hers, as if receiving communion. She smiles in admiration as she notices the napkin bears the Chanel logo.

"What's the deal?" Ralph asks James backstage.

"It's Dick's special talent. He makes a fantastic French 75. Everyone begs him for the recipe — even some of the local bartenders. But he won't let anyone in on his secret."

The crowd is still singing along with Dick as he rolls the tea cart off-stage. He smiles gratefully at James and collapses into a chair.

It doesn't take the judges long to proclaim Dick the winner of the Prohibition Pageant, which has raised more than $20,000 toward the restoration of Rehoboth's temperance fountain, not counting the "special dispensation" checks James slipped to each judge.

Ralph, Kissy, James, and the Holzstocks surround Dick as Miss Chanel Sweetbooty places a gaudy rhinestone tiara atop Dick's purple wig.

"Mwah! Mwah! I knew you could do it," Kissy exclaims, air-kissing Dick and everyone else within a two-foot radius.

James adds his congratulations, giving Dick a real kiss.

"James, you saved the day—again."

They're interrupted as the Pie Ladies bring over a magnum of Veuve Clicquot champagne from the bar. Everyone begins dancing as the DJ cranks up the volume for another round of "You're Just Too Good to Be True."

Just Another Day
at the Beach

*Poodle Beach gets some unlikely
visitors. Is Dick in over his head?*

"PLEASE LET US JOIN YOU. We've never been to Poodle Beach before." While on his way downtown to the big summer bathing suit sale at Timothy's Tog Shop, Dick Hunter has been cornered on the sidewalk by Ashley Holzstock.

"Well … uh … I'm not sure it's your scene."

"You might be wrong about that," Ashley says with a smile.

"It gets extremely crowded on weekends," he says, hoping to dissuade her. Dick doesn't like to entertain on the beach, preferring instead to read his *Vanity Fair* magazine and watch the buff bodies on display.

"Oh, don't worry about us. I don't mind crowds, and I assure you, my boy won't try to be top dog. We play well with others, really we do. It would be so fun. Pretty please?" Ashley bats her blue eyes.

"With sugar on top?"

"Fine, fine," Dick says quickly, looking around to make sure no one he knows is within earshot. "We'll be there tomorrow, near the hot dog stand. Look for our red-and-white striped beach umbrella."

Ashley gives him a hug and scampers off. Dick continues on to Timothy's Tog Shop, where James is already trying on bathing suits.

"Wow, look at you," Dick exclaims. James is standing before a full-length mirror in a red Speedo suit and a white t-shirt. "You look like a lifeguard."

"Um, thanks?"

"I just had a strange encounter with Ashley Holzstock," he tells James and gives him a little kiss. "She begged me to let them accompany us to Poodle Beach tomorrow. I said yes because I didn't see a way out of it."

"The Holzstocks at the gay beach? That will be interesting."

"Indeed."

"What do you think of the suit? I've always wanted a Speedo, but all the guys on the baseball team made fun of the men who wore them."

"If I were you, I'd do it now while you have the physique for it."

Dick and James notice that Timothy, the shop owner, has joined them.

"Red is perfect for your skin tone. And that particular cut offers a hint of reveal, which in your case—"

Dick clears his throat.

The shop owner turns. "Now what about you?" he asks Dick.

"I'm just here with him. My swimsuit is fine."

James makes a choking sound.

"What?" Dick glares at James.

"It must be ten years old!"

"It is not, why I bought it at—"

"We can't have that now, can we?" says Timothy. "Come, come. I have the perfect line of swimsuits for you. Trust me when I say these swimsuits are sophisticated and comfortable, and can take you from the beach to après la plage cocktails. But the best part is the flat waistband, which means no elastic pinching. It is a very flattering cut for us older gentlemen. I have them on sale today for $230."

"*On sale* for $230? That's outrageous."

Timothy shrugs his shoulders. "They're European."

THE SURF IS ROUGHER THAN NORMAL for this time of the summer, as Dick and James arrive at their usual spot on Poodle Beach. James sets up the red-and-white striped umbrella and matching chairs, being careful to tilt the umbrella into the wind.

Despite the less-than-stellar conditions, the beach is packed. If you want to understand gay

Rehoboth, Dick often says, there's no better place than Poodle Beach on a Saturday afternoon in the height of summer. You'll find young guys and old guys, those who are clean-cut and those who are tattooed. They come from Philly and Baltimore, DC and beyond, to swim and sun and read and run. Poodle Beach is the place where you can pick up either the latest town gossip or a play date for the afternoon.

James hands Dick a plastic tumbler full of his homemade sangria.

"Good Lord, it's worse than I imagined."

"It could have aged a little longer, but I don't think it's *that* bad," James says, tasting it himself.

"No, not the sangria. That!" Dick points toward two figures careening through the epicenter of Poodle Beach. Out in front is Ashley Holzstock in a white bikini, huge sunglasses, and a pair of white high heels. A large and out-of-control black poodle on a leash is dragging her forward over unsuspecting sunbathers and picnickers. Sand is flying everywhere and people are yelling. Behind her, and bearing a large "Bud Light" cooler on his shoulder, is husband Chip.

"We made it!" Chip drops to his knees, panting even more than the dog.

"Who is this?" James asks, as the poodle leaps wildly onto his leg.

"This is Pepe. I told you we'd fit in," Ashley says

triumphantly.

James rubs the dog's head. Dick stands back.

"Where are the other poodles?" Ashley asks, looking around the beach while James tries to escape from Pepe's grasp, fearful the ill-behaved dog is about to start humping his leg.

"What do you mean?" Dick asks.

"This is Poodle Beach, right? So where are the poodles?"

Ashley and Chip stare at Dick, waiting for an answer.

"Wait. You're serious?"

Now the couple looks confused.

"Oh yes, I can tell now that you are." After a short pause, Dick looks around. "Hmm. It *is* odd. I don't see any other poodles on the beach today. Perhaps it's too windy? But take a seat. James has packed a marvelous picnic lunch. And we have his special homemade sangria."

As they set up their chairs and blankets, Chip asks James to rub sunscreen on his back. "Ashley won't do it unless I've waxed. Couldn't get an appointment this week."

"The hair and the lotion get all icky," she says.

All eyes on Poodle watch James Flores, wearing his new, red Speedo, rub lotion on the newcomer. "Go lower," Chip instructs, puffing up his chest and twisting his torso left and right like a Greek God being anointed with oil.

James works his hands down Chip's lower back, finishing up by running his finger around the inside of the man's swimsuit. Were it not for the rough surf, James knew the voyeurs would have heard the yelp from a surprised Chip Holzstock.

Dick, meanwhile, is explaining the origin of the name "Poodle Beach."

"Nobody is sure exactly how the name came about. Some say it's because all the gay guys sit on the beach coiffed and groomed, much like poodles. Then there's the two cousins theory: two cousins from Maryland would drive here every weekend in a big Cadillac convertible, and when they got to the beach, they'd bring out their poodle dogs and set up camp."

He looks at Ashley to see if his message is sinking in.

"So people don't really bring their poodles?"

"No, not usually."

"Now don't I feel silly."

ASHLEY MAY HAVE FELT SILLY, but Dick felt ridiculous. Everyone had warned him not to go in the water, but he could not be dissuaded. Neither rough conditions nor cold temperatures would stop Dick Hunter from taking his customary dip.

He hadn't, however, expected such a strong undertow. Then he was hit by an incoming wave — not even a big one. The combination knocked him off-balance and caused him to twist into an uncomfortable position. He had managed to keep his balance, but he pulled something in his leg that now made it virtually impossible to walk.

Dick retreats to deeper water, where it is easier to maneuver. *What to do.* He needs assistance, but James is in deep conversation with Ashley, who seems never to stop talking.

Dick finally is able to catch James's attention and beckons to him. James shakes his head. Dick gestures again, adding a look of desperation. Finally recognizing that something might not be right, James wades in and makes his way out to Dick, who explains his predicament.

"I'll just escort you out. Lean on me."

"I'll do no such thing. I cannot have you come rescue your infirm boyfriend who went in the surf despite everyone's advising against it. The vicious queens on Poodle Beach will have a field day with me."

"You're not infirm. Tell me, though, how do you plan to walk out?"

"Wait until they all leave? I don't know. That's why I called you."

"I have an idea."

"I thought sure you would."

James returns to shore and grabs something from the beach bag. He carefully makes his way back out to Dick.

"I've got the waterproof camera. I'm thinking we'll pretend to be taking selfies with the big waves. It will give us an excuse to lock arms, and you can lean on me while we walk out."

"It could work."

"It *will* work."

Together, they make their way out of the water and up onto the beach, snapping photos along the way. When they finally arrive at their spot, they snap one last selfie before slowly lowering themselves, arm-in-arm, into their beach chairs. Dick sits back, bracing his sore leg with a mound of sand on each side. James wraps some ice from the cooler in a towel and places it on the strain—an old baseball remedy he knew would quickly get Dick back on his feet.

"James, what would I do without you?"

"Crawl out on your hands and knees?"

"I'd have drowned first."

A Most Unusual Sweet Potato Competition

Dick and James go to the fair and get into a jam.

"WHY ARE WATERMELONS HERE WITH THE VEGETABLES instead of over with the peaches, pears, and plums?" Dick asks James as they watch Judge Betty Regina present the award ribbons for the heaviest watermelon.

Dick and James are standing inside the new 16,000-square-foot, metal-framed, agriculture hall on the grounds of the Delaware State Fair. The scent of fresh sawdust on the floor tickles their noses as they wait impatiently for the Most Unusual Sweet Potato Competition. It is about to begin, after a substantial delay that occurred after one of the watermelons rolled off its stand and onto the foot of the esteemed fruit and vegetable judge.

"Watermelons have the characteristics of both a fruit and a vegetable," James explains nonchalantly, as Fritz Wilmerding joins them.

"Are you saying that watermelons are bisexual?" Fritz asks.

"Most watermelons produce both male and female flowers, so I'd say they're more hermaphroditic," James answers.

"James, how do you know these things?" Dick looks at him in admiration.

"It's sort of the family business."

"Oh, right," says Dick. "Did you know Wallis Simpson was rumored to be a hermaphrodite?"

"Who?" James looks puzzled.

"Hush! Here comes the judge." Fritz Wilmerding lifts a finger to his lips as Judge Betty Regina, resplendent in a dark-green, taffeta gown, limps toward the hundred or so people gathered around the tubers on display.

The Most Unusual Sweet Potato Competition is one of the more popular produce contests at the State Fair, along with the heaviest watermelon and the prettiest tomato. For some reason, amateur gardeners are wild for all the crazy shapes the sweet potato can morph into while growing underground.

Dick looks around at the teeming mass of humanity in the agriculture hall and shakes the sawdust from his Gucci loafers. Never in his wildest imagination would he ever have considered venturing into this festival of farmers, fatties, and fried foods on a Friday night. But Fritz Wilmerding was a true friend and a true fan of the sweet potato. Sweet potato fries were the secret behind the Wilmerding family's french fry business. Fritz grew them not because he liked them—he didn't—but because he had a warped sense of family pride.

"C'est parti," Fritz whispers to his friends as Judge Betty Regina instructs each contestant to please stand with his or her entry. He runs his hands down his too-tight madras plaid jacket to smooth out the wrinkles and adjusts his bow tie before stepping behind his red-speckled, Georgia Jet sweet potato, which is shaped like a heart—not a real one, but a classic Valentine's Day heart. He stands proudly, waiting for the judge to get to his entry.

"This might be his year," Dick whispers to James. "Last summer, he entered a small sweet potato covered with fine roots. It looked exactly like a kiwi fruit. Fritz felt certain it was unusual enough to place in the competition, but Judge Betty Regina apparently thought otherwise. A couple of years before that, he raised a large, purple sweet potato that bore an uncanny resemblance to the legendary phallus of Jeff Stryker."

"Who?"

Dick rolls his eyes, not even bothering to explain the reference to the porn star. "Of course, the competition jury rejected that sweet potato as not family friendly. Fritz, you can imagine, was furious, especially given the homage to animal husbandry throughout the fairgrounds."

Dick and James watch Judge Betty Regina methodically move from one end of the entries to the other, picking up each sweet potato in the process and rolling it between her hands before bringing it up close to her trained eye for a better look.

"She thinks this is the Westminster Dog Show," Dick mumbles a little too loudly.

After completing her very thorough review of all twelve sweet potatoes in the competition, Judge Betty Regina snaps her fingers and a tall, goofy-looking boy comes running with a tray containing the prize ribbons. She picks up the yellow fourth-place ribbon and quickly places it on an orangish sweet potato that resembles an ear. Dick felt it was more impressive than the third place winner—a potato that was supposed to look like a Gorbachev troika doll, complete with birthmark, although, try as he might, Dick couldn't see the resemblance.

The crowd is on its toes as Judge Betty Regina picks up the red, second-place ribbon and limps slowly toward the far end of the line of contestants, where she hands it with little fanfare to Alma Bean, a lean, tight-lipped woman whose copper-colored sweet potato resembles a nesting hen. Loud gasps of disbelief from Alma's friends and family echo through the metal building. Alma Bean—avid gardener and long-standing member of the Hardscrabble Free Will Baptist Church—had won this contest each of the last six years and three times before that. She collapses into the arms of her sister Beulah, too stunned to speak, but nevertheless clutching the red, second-place ribbon to her chest, while Judge Betty Regina walks away.

Several of the Baptists boo. Beulah begins to sob. Alma's oldest son picks up his mama's sweet potato and hurls it at Judge Betty Regina, barely missing the judge's head.

Nonplussed by the racket made by the Bean family and friends, Judge Betty Regina lifts the final award ribbon above her head and does a slow twirl, so everyone in the audience can get a good glimpse of the plus-sized blue ribbon *and* her green gown. Taffeta rustling, she strides over and presents the first-prize award to Fritz Wilmerding, who lets out a whoop of delight and executes a perfect curtsy upon acceptance. A representative from Smyrna Seed and Feed, the competition's main sponsor, hands Fritz a check for $250.

A photographer quickly ushers judge and winner together for a photo. A reporter from the *Downstate Gazette* asks Fritz how it feels to upset the mighty Alma Bean, saying, "You know, some people believe Jesus Christ Himself has a hand in growing her sweet potatoes."

"Well, all I can say is that Jesus must have loved the music I played for my sweet potatoes." Fritz holds up the winning, heart-shaped tuber. "Don't look all surprised because I serenade my plants."

Fritz winks at the young male reporter. "Music inspires them to grow. I played Schumann exclusively this summer. He was such a romantic, and totally obsessed with his young piano accompanist. I know *exactly* how he felt. Every time I look at the butt on that new bartender at Azul when he fetches me a cocktail, another dollar jumps out of my wallet."

The reporter stops scribbling in his notepad and looks up at Fritz.

"You don't have to write down that last part," Dick says.

After a few more questions and plenty of congratulations from well-wishers delighted to have witnessed the dethroning of Alma Bean, the three men leave the building in high spirits. The Bean family, on the other hand, huddles nearby, still not believing what they heard. Alma Bean losing to a homosexual from Rehoboth Beach was quite simply a travesty. The sinner surely paid off the judge, they whisper knowingly among themselves.

DICK, JAMES, AND FRITZ ARE IN HIGH SPIRITS. Fritz is sporting the blue ribbon on the lapel of his madras jacket. Award ribbons are supposed to stay with the winning vegetables until the fair ends, but Fritz snatched it when nobody was looking, or so he thought. Though Judge Betty Regina and the crowd of prize vegetable groupies had moved on to the Best Burpless Cucumber Competition, several members of the still-stunned Bean family had witnessed Fritz's transgression. They shook their heads. It was further proof of the amoral occurrence that had just transpired.

"Tis a splendid summer evening for exploring the fair," Fritz declares, linking arms with his friends as they stroll the midway.

"Must we?" Dick whines.

Fritz stops and, with hands on hips, looks his friend up and down. "Dick Hunter, you are such a snob."

Dick gazes at a sign that says, "This Way to the Racing Pigs."

Dick and James grudgingly accompany Fritz to the 4-H pavilion, where they ogle some cute farm boys and their Billy goats and see some exotic-looking chickens. Finally, the Rehobothians arrive at Fritz's proclaimed favorite part of the fair.

"You don't see many freak shows in today's politically-correct society," Fritz says to his friends as they stand in front of a painted wooden sign advertising, "The One and Only Living Snake Lady," Miss Linda L'Amor.

According to Fritz, there are only four such exhibits at the Delaware State Fair besides Linda the Snake Lady: a twenty-nine-inch woman, the world's tiniest horse, Gorilla Man, and a Museum of Oddities with two-headed chickens, shrunken heads, and space-alien babies.

"Egad, I could really use a cocktail right now," Dick says.

Fritz reaches into the breast pocket of his jacket and slowly withdraws a flat silver flask. "Then you are in luck. The fair may be dry, gentlemen, but Fritz Wilmerding is not. I came prepared with a small supply of good bourbon."

"I'll go get us some Cokes," James announces.

"And some of those fried Oreos, if you will," Fritz calls after James.

"C'mon, let's go." Fritz pulls a reluctant Dick to the ticket booth, where they pay the admission fee for Linda the Snake Lady and then proceed into a curtained room that contains a makeshift wooden cage covered by chicken wire. The ubiquitous State Fair sawdust covers the floor.

Dick observes the snake lady, who is advertised as having the head of a beautiful girl and the body of an ugly snake. A woman's head is sticking up from a hole in the bottom of the cage and is "attached" to the body of a five-foot-long taxidermy snake. Her pale-blue eyes are blinking rapidly, and her tongue is flicking in and out.

"I wouldn't exactly call her beautiful," Dick says. "With that crooked grin and all that frizzy blonde hair, she looks a little cuckoo."

"Hush." Fritz punches Dick on the arm. "She might hear you."

"Hello there, Fritzie," Linda speaks. Her voice is low and gravelly. "I was hoping you'd come by to see me this year."

"You know I always swing by to see my favorite serpent." Fritz and Linda share a chuckle.

Dick looks on, dumbfounded. "Fritz, you might have. . . ."

"How's the season so far?" Fritz asks the snake lady.

"Made a lot of money in Raleigh. Richmond was a washout on account of all the rain. We're heading to Harrisburg next week. Who's that tall drink of water with you?"

"Pardonnez moi. Ms. Linda L'Amor, I'd like to present my oldest and dearest friend, Mr. Dick Hunter." Fritz extends his arm from Dick to Linda in an exaggerated manner. "We met in college and were boyfriends for a while until that got boring."

"That your real name, hon?" She laughs and then coughs. "Good advertising for a homo." Dick winces.

"Linda and I met when I began entering the sweet potato competition," Fritz starts to explain, but is interrupted when a mother and two little boys approach the cage.

She snaps into character. "Hi there, my name's

Linda, and I am half woman, half Burmese python. You can come closer, but please, no pictures. He don't like it." She gestures with her head toward the tattooed man selling tickets.

With a new rapt audience, she tells the story of how her parents were missionaries in Borneo in the 1950s and her pregnant mama was exposed to some experimental drugs left over from World War II. Her mother died giving birth, and her father ran off after seeing the snake child slither out.

"The good nuns in Borneo named me Linda because I'm a beautiful gift from God. They taught me to speak and to read. Of course, I can't write cuz I ain't got arms, but I can do some math in my head. It's important to learn your math, you hear me?"

The little boys are too spellbound to speak. They shriek and run off when Linda flicks her tongue and tells them she eats white mice and small children.

"That's some spiel," Dick says with a laugh. "You do know that Burmese pythons don't live on Borneo."

She flicks her tongue at him.

"So tell me again, Linda, how exactly did you meet Fritz?"

"Me and him was both screwing the boy who deep-fried the Oreos."

"Excuse me?" Dick looks over at Fritz, who shrugs his shoulders.

"It's true, I'm afraid. Linda walked in one night and caught us in flagrante Oreo."

"Shoot, I weren't mad or nothin' cuz everyone knew Cecil—that was his name—couldn't keep that big thing in his pants."

"We shared him for the remainder of the fair," Fritz adds, a faraway look in his eyes.

"Now Fritzie comes to see me every summer." Linda laughs and coughs. "Hey, Fritzie, how about a snort? You bring some hooch? It's awful hot in this here cage." Linda flicks her tongue.

Fritz snaps out of his daydream and brandishes the silver flask. "Ta-da! You ready?"

"Does a fat dog fart?" Linda tilts her head back and opens her mouth wide, like an oversized baby bird ready for the worm.

"Oh, this is just too tawdry! I must get a photo of this or no one will believe me." Dick pulls out his phone and motions for Fritz to stand closer to the cage as he sets up the photo.

All of a sudden, Fritz and Dick are grabbed from behind.

"Hey!" Linda yells, as two men wearing Philadelphia Eagles football jerseys grapple with Dick and Fritz. The smaller of the two punches Dick in the stomach.

The big one, whose jersey has "11" and the name "Tebow" printed on it, waves an open pocketknife in their faces. "Don't move."

"What, pray tell, do you mean by attacking us like that, Tebow?" Fritz challenges the big man, as small, yippy dogs are oft to do. "I realize the sign said no photos of Linda are allowed, but she told us it would be OK."

Dick remains hunched over, trying to catch his breath.

"What the hell you talkin' 'bout?" Tebow scowls at Fritz.

"We were getting ready to enjoy a cocktail with Miss Linda L'Amor when you two goons interrupted our little party."

"Technically, that wasn't a cocktail," Dick manages to get in between gasps of breath.

"Listen, you old fairy," Tebow interrupts, pointing at Fritz, "this ain't got nutin' to do with that snake girl. This is about you bribin' that judge and stealin' first prize for the sweet potato."

"I did no such thing," says Fritz, "and I'm shocked you would imply wrongdoing. Betty Regina is a fine, upstanding judge whose ethics and reputation are beyond reproach. I'll have you brainless Baptists know, I won that contest fair and square."

"Bullshit. That judge is in your queer pocket, and everyone knows it. Our poor mama is laid up in the first aid tent over behind the funnel cake stand. She's delirious and speaking in tongues."

"Isn't that a good thing for you people?" Fritz shoots back.

"Shut up. Me and Brilliant here want that prize back."

"'Brilliant'? What kind of name is that?" Fritz can't help but exclaim.

"Mama named me Brilliant cuz I'm the light of her life," the smaller man says with a bragging tone he has clearly used before. "See, here's my driver's license." He starts to take out his wallet.

"Stop that!" Tebow grabs his younger brother's arm. "We don't want them knowin' who we are."

"As if we didn't already," Fritz mumbles.

Tebow turns back to Fritz and points the knife at him. "You shut up. Mama was countin' on that prize money to put in her fall cabbages and cauliflowers. That money is rightfully hers, and we want it back."

"If that's all you want," Fritz cries out, "take the bloody check." He reaches into his jacket and tosses it at the big man. "Just let us be."

"Check ain't no good to me," Tebow snarls, but he picks it up. "I want cash."

"Well, I don't have any. You can have the blue ribbon."

"Don't want the darn ribbon." Tebow snatches it off Fritz's lapel and tosses it at Dick.

"You look rich." Which, of course, Dick does, attired in a classic, navy blazer, lavender, tailored shorts, and a heavily starched, button-down shirt. "Gimme your wallet."

Dick complies.

"God damn, it's empty. Don't you ladies carry any money?"

"Cash is so passé." Fritz yawns. "Perhaps even déclassé."

Tebow removes a bankcard from Dick's wallet and waves it in front of his face. "You got a card here. Brilliant can just go to the ATM machine and take out some cash while I keep watch here."

"You do realize the use of the word "machine" in the context of ATM is redundant," Fritz says.

"Shuddup!" I ain't talkin' to you."

Tebow turns back to Dick. "Now, gimme the PIN number!"

"Redundant!" Fritz yells.

"I *said* what's your PIN number?" Tebow glares at Dick.

"I don't understand," Dick replies.

"The number for your card."

"It's on the front."

"No, mo-ron, I want the PIN number! Your secret code." Tebow is starting to get red in the face.

"I'm sorry, but I don't believe I have a secret code."

"Bullshit. Everyone has one."

"And I'm telling you I don't."

"How do you get cash?" Tebow asks.

"I go to the bank."

"Exactly. So what's your PIN number?"

"I don't know."

Fritz interrupts the interrogation. "Hold on, brilliant. Dick here is what you call 'old money.'"

"I ain't Brilliant, he's Brilliant." Tebow points to his smaller brother.

Fritz and Dick give each other a smile.

"What I was saying," Fritz continues, "is that Dick prefers to bank with a human teller, not an *automated teller machine*."

"Goddamn, smartass fairy!" Tebow slaps Fritz across the face.

At nearly the same moment, a familiar-looking, well-sculpted man brandishing a tennis racquet leaps into the arena, and with a forehand swing that would make Roger Federer proud, knocks the knife out of Tebow's hand. He follows it up with a perfect backhand to Tebow's head, which sends the man tumbling. During the commotion, Brilliant tries to make a break for it.

"Not so fast."

"Bravo! Bravo!" Linda yells from her cage.

"James to the rescue!" Fritz adds.

Within seconds, the Delaware state police show up on the scene and apprehend Tebow and not-so-Brilliant.

"The guy taking tickets tipped me off," James explains. "So I called the cops."

Where'd you get a tennis racquet?" Dick asks. "I thought you went for drinks."

"And Oreos," Fritz adds.

"I was on my way back with the Cokes and fried Oreos when I saw a tennis display."

"At the fair?" Dick exclaims.

"Over with the hot tubs and gutter guards. Who knew? Anyhow, I've had my eye on this new racquet for some time. And it was on sale, so. . . ."

Linda chuckles as the police take their prisoners away. "Who is this stud muffin?" she asks, giving James the once-over.

"Young James here is Dick's current paramour," Fritz explains.

"Hell of an upgrade, if you ask me," Linda says.

"Which nobody did," Fritz snaps back.

"Oh, Fritzie, don't get all hot and bothered. Now how about that drink? And a fried Oreo for old time's sake."

James looks at Dick.

"Don't ask. But I must commemorate this," Dick says, and begins to arrange everyone beside the cage for a photo.

James is posed, holding the tennis racquet. Fritz holds up the blue ribbon and the flask. A brown bag of fried Oreos sits atop the cage, grease staining the paper. Linda smiles broadly.

"OK now — 1, 2, 3 — Say 'sweet potato.'"

"Sweet potato," they all yell.

Of Sound Mind and Disposition

*Dick wants to update his will, but
not everyone is pleased.*

IT IS A SERIOUS AND PURPOSEFUL DICK
HUNTER who bicycles the half-mile from his
cottage on Pine Cone Lane to the home of his older
sister Jane, who has been residing—hiding out
is more like it—in the Henlopen Acres section of
Rehoboth Beach. Technically a self-governing town,
"The Acres" is one of the wealthiest and snobbiest
enclaves in Delaware. It is perfect for dear Jane.

After having been attacked at the State Fair, Dick
took the incident as a sign and decided to update
his will, something he hadn't done since his divorce, more than a decade ago.

His desire to make a provision in it for James
had been reported to his sister by the loose-lipped
Pru Pennypacker—the family's longtime money manager at the very blue blood Greene Brothers in Philadelphia. Jane then had made a mission
out of trying to get Dick to change his mind and

leave James out of the will. Following yet another rambling, late-night phone call on the topic from a gin-sodden Jane, Dick had decided enough was enough.

Desiring an element of surprise for the encounter, Dick arrives extremely early on a Sunday morning. He finds the spare key Jane keeps hidden beneath one of the nineteenth-century, hunting-dog statues gracing the front porch. Quietly, he enters the English Tudor-style home, disarms the alarm system with its predictable code, and sneaks up on Jane, who is sleeping soundly in the enormous master bedroom. Humming a line from the Virginia football touchdown song loudly into his sterling silver kazoo, he rouses his sister, who bolts upright, screams, and swings a pillow at her brother.

"What the hell are you doing?"

"Payback, dear sis." Wahoo wah! He blows the kazoo at her again. "Your late-night phone diatribes will cease and desist immediately. I mean it."

It takes Jane a minute to realize what Dick is talking about. "Oh, that. Well, go fix me a bloody mary. There's a bottle of Pepto-Bismol in the fridge — bring that, too. And put that damn kazoo away; you're not a member of the pep band anymore."

Dick fetches both requested hangover remedies for his sister and slams them down on a bedside table, causing Jane to jump again.

"What I do with my money is my business," Dick begins, "and I want to do something nice for James."

"But Dick, he's a gold digger."

"No, he digs *me*," Dick says, adding, "so technically he's a Dick digger." He pauses. The retort hadn't sounded as convincing as he had intended.

"Be serious." Jane takes a long sip of the bloody mary. "The boy has weaseled his way into your life, and now he's trying to weasel his way into your bank account."

"James is an earnest and honest young man who has never asked me for one single dime. Changing the will is *my* idea."

"He works in a common gym," Jane replies, her nose crinkling.

"And he makes good money as a personal trainer. There is a waiting list for his services."

"And which services are those?"

"He's a godsend."

"Dick, listen to me. It's bad enough you are so public with your lifestyle. Can't you at least find someone more appropriate? I hear his family picks watermelons."

"Who told you that?

"I can't remember."

"Well, it's really no one else's business, but the Flores family are hard-working farmers who, yes, at times have picked watermelons. You do realize that someone needs to do that in order for you to have your watermelon martinis?"

"I do not drink—"

"And your society husband picked people's pockets, so you hardly have room to talk. He bilked over three million dollars from your trust fund, and you still haven't divorced the cad."

"Big Nat just made a bad investment is all."

"He's in prison!"

Jane's husband, Nathaniel Stoutbury III—known as Big Nat—had been born with a silver spoon in his mouth, the great-grandson of a prominent Philadelphia banker and coal financier. Big Nat fancied himself as an angel investor. The problem was, he had a knack for picking losing ventures. His gamble on a wind energy farm off the Delaware Coast had seemed like a winner until the recession hit. He began forging checks from Jane's trust account to keep funding the investment and their lifestyle.

"Seriously, Dick, what, besides your money, could the boy possibly be interested in?"

"Well, if you must know, he says I'm good in the sack."

Jane stares at him with a slack-jawed expression.

"Close your mouth, Jane. That was a joke."

Dick realizes he shouldn't even waste his breath trying to explain his relationship with James to someone like Jane, who has never strayed from the conventional mores she has grown up with. "We have fun together, and I'm happy. Why can't you be happy for my happiness?"

"Enough with the goddamn happiness. You sound like one of the silly self-help addicts in my book club. I'm just trying to look out for your best interests. I always have," Jane says, with a toothy smile.

"And I appreciate that, I really do." Dick smiles back. "But I've thought about this, and nothing you can say will make me change my mind, so please quit pestering me."

"Very well, but don't say I didn't try to warn you. Now walk away, please," Jane orders with a wave of her hand. "I need peace and quiet so my morning medicine will kick in."

Dick blows the kazoo once more as he departs.

A FEW WEEKS LATER, JANE is in the office of dentist Rodney Snapp, who nonchalantly asks about her brother Dick.

"The fool is changing his will to accommodate that gold digger," she mumbles incoherently. "Ouch! That hurts."

"So sorry, Jane. My hand slipped. What did you say?"

"I said he's changing his will to include that Mexican boy. I tried to talk some sense into him, but what can I do?"

After a few minutes of silence and the sound of air sucking saliva from Jane's mouth, Red Snapper finally speaks. "You're a clever girl. Why don't you simply replace the will with a forged one that doesn't include the interloper?"

Jane brushes his hand away from her mouth. "How can I do that?"

"It's quite simple. Start by calling Willis Wythe."

"The artist?"

"He's a dear friend of mine. Identify yourself and tell him I recommended his talent. Be sure to use those exact words, 'recommended his talent.'"

"I don't understand."

"Willis has great skill with detail and in replication. He can copy anything, if you get my drift. He'll invite you to his studio where you can explain your predicament."

"I can't ask a stranger to commit forgery."

"Well, don't act all high and holy. Everyone knows your husband is in jail."

"And I don't want to join him."

"You won't. Willis is discreet and completely trustworthy. Everyone uses his services."

"Like who?"

"As I said, he is discreet, and so am I. He will give you what you need, and all you have to do is purchase one of his paintings."

"Must I?"

"In advance."

"In advance? But they're *so* expensive."

"God, you're tight as a tick, Jane. I am merely offering a simple solution to your problem."

"And I appreciate it."

"Then pay a visit to Willis."

Jane nods in affirmation. "It might work. I'm certain I can convince Pru Pennypacker at Greene Brothers to replace the will. She's no friend of James."

"You know, Pru is a dear client of mine, too. Now how about I whiten those pretty teeth of yours? Too much red wine is not a friend to white enamel."

Before Jane can complain about the expense, Red Snapper tells her it's on the house. A small price, he thinks, to help her stick it to Dick Hunter.

"I ABSOLUTELY LOVE THIS PAINTING," Dick exclaims, stepping back and admiring the depiction of a well-appointed, late eighteenth-century gentleman's salon.

"It's called 'His Quarters,' by Willis Wythe," Jane explains. "I hope you'll keep it. I don't know what Big Nat saw in it when he bought it, but my decorator would dump me as a client if I displayed this nonsense."

"So nice of you."

"And so nice of you to invite me to dinner."

"Well, burying the hatchet and all that."

As James brings out the dinner course, Jane excuses herself to phone her son Little Nat, who, she explains, is having a decorating crisis. She quietly enters Dick's study and begins rummaging through his desk drawers in search of his will.

"Jane," she hears Dick calling, "your dinner is getting cold."

"Damn it," she mutters, hurrying back to the dining room to take her seat. "So sorry about that. Little Nat is wallpapering his condo and can't decide between pagodas and butterflies."

Dick and James give her a confused look.

"They're both wallpaper patterns," Jane rattles on, "and I told him he can't go wrong with either. Tell me, James, how did you prepare this delicious chicken?"

"It's very simple. I rub it with olive oil and crushed garlic, and then stuff it with lemons. The secret is to slow-roast it in a terra cotta covered dish."

"Will you excuse me for another moment?" Jane interrupts the cooking lesson and gets up from the table. She walks down the hallway to the guest powder room and turns on the light and the overhead fan. Then, she closes the door and tiptoes farther down the hall to Dick's study. She scans the room, looking for places where Dick might store a will, until she spies an antique strongbox high up on one of the book-laden shelves.

She takes it down. Of course it's not locked, and she laughs at Dick's naiveté. She rifles through its contents: a copy of Dick's divorce papers, gold wedding band, Society of the Cincinnati rosette, some family photos, birth certificate, passport, and several roach clips. Jane gives them a closer look and realizes they are nothing but old paperclip prototypes from the family's manufacturing business. Just as she grabs the creamy-white Greene Brothers envelope that almost certainly contains the will, she hears someone coming down the hallway toward the study. She quickly dives under the desk with the strongbox.

On his way to the unoccupied bathroom in Dick's study, James can't help but see Jane's feet sticking out from under the desk. Otis, the old basset hound, is sniffing at them.

"Well, what do we have here? The Wicked Witch of the East? No ruby slippers, though; just a pair of Belgian loafers. Jane, what are you doing down there?"

After an uncomfortably long pause, Jane replies that she's looking for a wedding ring and pulls herself up off the floor, putting the strongbox on the desk. "Little Nat is getting married."

"Congratulations."

"If only. The girl is Jewish, and her overbearing father wants them to wear silver wedding bands, which just won't do. I thought if I could offer a gold Hunter family ring for Little Nat, I might prevent this travesty."

"Why didn't you simply ask Dick?"

"Well, the way things have been going between us, I was certain he would say no."

"So you were just going to steal it?"

"It's not like he'll be needing it."

"What makes you so sure of that?"

Jane blanches, but quickly recovers.

"I know it's terrible of me." She pretends to cry, peering through the fingers of the right hand covering her face to catch James's reaction.

James puts a muscled arm around her shoulder. "C'mon, let's go back to the dining room." James pries the envelope and the ring from Jane's hand and replaces them in the strongbox and returns it to the shelf.

Jane gazes at the box longingly over her shoulder as James leads her out of the study.

Back at the dinner table, James announces that Jane has some news. Dick looks at his sister.

"Little Nat is getting married."

"Well now, this certainly calls for a celebration. Who's the lucky girl?"

"A Jewess from New York. Her father is a prominent surgeon at Mount Sinai Hospital. They're getting married in East Hampton next summer."

"I take it from the tone of your voice you don't approve."

"My grandchildren will be Jews. My husband is in jail. And my brother is a practicing homosexual. This isn't what the Hunter family aspires to."

"Actually—" Dick begins a counter response, but James interrupts him.

"I have an idea. Dick, why don't you offer Little Nat your grandfather's wedding ring. You've always been fond of him, and you still have the ring, don't you?" He gives Jane a wink.

"I do. I'm not sure, though. Supposing you and I—"

"We'll get new rings. Matching ones. And besides, Jane did give us that fabulous Willis Wythe painting, and we know it wasn't cheap." James gestures toward the heavily framed painting resting against the wall.

"No, it wasn't," says Jane, and then mumbles "and some good buying it did me."

"Of course, you're right. I'll give the ring to Little Nat myself. Jane, it would be an honor to continue the Hunter tradition. I hope you'll accept the offer."

"Yes, thank you," Jane says, through a forced smile.

At this, James pops the cork on a bottle of Veuve Clicquot and fills their glasses. He watches Jane as he raises his glass and toasts, "Where there's a will, there's a way!"

Jane's face loses a little color.

As they clink their glasses together, James starts to form a plan. He won't tell Dick about Jane's attempt to steal from the strongbox just yet. He knows how much Dick dislikes family discord. Sister Jane, he senses, is up to something. He'd have to keep a closer eye on her from here on out.

The Big Blow

*A hurricane is coming. Will we
see Dick and James run?*

"A STORM OF BIBLICAL PROPORTIONS!" Fritz Wilmerding's voice is cracking, and he's gyrating like a Pentecostal at a gay wedding as he barges through the front door of Dick Hunter's home.

"For goodness sake, Fritz, calm down." Dick holds out a bottle of bourbon in an effort to ward off his friend's demonic advance. "I was just about to fix myself a mid-morning cocktail. Would you like one?"

It was an affectation passed down from Dick's grandfather who, like many men on Wall Street back in the day, often slipped away before lunch for a toddy or two. It was said to shore up one's moral fiber. Dick often needed a little fortification while working on one of his writing projects.

Fritz grabs the bourbon bottle and takes a healthy swig. "There's no time for lollygagging. We've got to get ready. This hurricane looks like a doozy."

Dick knows Fritz is prone to exaggeration. Never let the truth stand in the way of a good story has always been Fritz's personal motto.

"Why haven't I heard anything about this hurricane?" Dick grabs the bottle back from his agitated friend.

"Because you don't watch the Weather Channel."

"True. I find the network's coverage histrionic. It disturbs me that they now give every common winter storm some ridiculous name like Ajax or Goliath."

"Dick Hunter, step off your soap box. Hurricane Chester is a category 3, and they say it's poised to deliver a bull's-eye hit on the Delaware Coast." Fritz is panting, and his eyes are beginning to bulge out of their sockets.

"The hurricane is named Chester?" Dick asks.

"I know, isn't it terrible? I envision a fat redneck in an Alabama sunsuit," Fritz replies. "The name is more fitting for a storm threatening the Gulf Coast rather than the East Coast, don't you think?"

"What, pray tell, is an Alabama sunsuit?"

"Overalls with nothing underneath."

"I can't imagine. No, actually, I can. Egads. But if I recall my Latin studies," Dick begins, "the name 'Chester' stems from the word *castra*, which means camp or fort."

"Rehoboth was founded by the Methodists as a spiritual resort *camp*," Fritz gasps. "And *Fort* Miles was built on the bluffs to watch for German subs

116

during World War II. It's a sign."

Dick hands his friend the bourbon bottle and pushes him down into a chair. "Drink."

Fritz gulps as if he has just eaten a jalapeno pepper.

"Rehoboth has never taken a direct hit from a hurricane," Dick says, sitting down beside his friend. "You've lived here long enough to know these storms always bounce off the Carolinas and pass us by. I'm convinced it's because of our geography. Delaware is tucked back from the rest of the coast like a weak chin."

"The great storm of 1962 wrecked all of Dad's french fry concession stands."

"It hurt a lot more than your family's french fries. And technically, that was a Nor'easter, not a hurricane."

"You say tomato I say tomahto. Still, we must prepare. I've made a checklist."

Fritz hands the list to Dick, who begins to read: "Band-Aids, antiseptic wipes, toilet paper, radio — do they even make radios anymore? Flashlight, batteries, cocktail shaker ... *cocktail shaker?*"

"For the party, of course."

"What party?"

"Your hurricane party."

"Oh, right. Wait a minute. Who says I'm having a hurricane party?" Dick grabs back the bourbon bottle.

"Don't be silly. Your house is the *only* place for

a hurricane party. It's not too close to the beach, so there's no danger of us drowning in the storm surge. It's well-built, so the roof won't blow off. God knows what will happen to mine — those poor old shingles — I get leaks every time it rains. But, most importantly, you have the best stocked bar in town."

"Had," Dick mutters, eyeing the now-empty bottle of bourbon.

🥂

"WE'LL BESTER CHESTER." "STAY AWAY CHESTER." Dick and James are strolling around downtown Rehoboth later that day, looking at all the clever messages scrawled on the sheets of plywood put up to protect glass windows and doors from the impending hurricane.

"Funny to think there's a storm lurking somewhere out there." James gestures to the dazzling blue sky.

On the horizon, though, Dick can see a small procession of wispy, white, cirrus clouds — the outer bands of the storm system predicted to make landfall near the mouth of the Delaware Bay.

They stop in front of Dom's, a popular Italian deli on Baltimore Avenue, where owner Dom Orso is outside stenciling, "Half price on all soft cheeses" on the plywood covering the establishment's big picture window. Frank Sinatra's "Stormy Weather" is playing inside the store.

"Are you planning to ride out the hurricane?" Dick asks the burly merchant.

"Of course. I have a generator. I'll cram everything into the walk-in coolers and duct tape them shut. If worse comes to worst and the generator fails, I can always survive on prosciutto and Parmesan. What about you guys?"

"I've put on the hurricane shutters," James replies, "but I need to drive out to Home Depot for some more supplies. I hear they're already seeing runs on coolers and tarps."

"I'm certain the Giant has been stripped of milk and bread," Dick adds, shaking his head. He's never understood why people feel compelled to stock up on milk and bread in advance of a storm. He supposed he would need to venture to a grocery store, whether he liked it or not.

The two men continue their stroll, carrying a nice paglietta cheese Dom gave them, stopping now and then to chat with acquaintances who are also out and about checking the storm preparations. Finally, they arrive at the lifeguard station on the boardwalk. Two square, red hurricane flags wave in the gentle breeze, and a crowd is gathered around a white Weather Channel van.

Fritz is among the throngs, and upon seeing Dick

and James, he begins frantically gesturing them over. At that moment, the van door slides open and out steps Strohm Chase, aka "Storm Chaser," the toothy, blond superhero of weather reporting.

James tugs at Dick. "That's definitely not a good sign. You know his motto is, 'Wherever the storm goes, Storm goes.' We should go meet him."

"Must we?"

"Don't be that way. It's not like we get a lot of stars coming through Rehoboth, except for Hoda and Kathie Lee, of course."

"Weather forecasters are now considered stars?"

"Dick, Storm has his own website, Facebook fan page, and over three hundred thousand Twitter followers. Besides, he's pretty hot, don't you think?"

"I suppose so, if you like men who look like golden retrievers."

As they make their way toward the van, Fritz rushes over to meet them. "Come with me. I want to introduce you to Storm. I've been following him all day. I even invited him to our party."

"*Our* party?"

"Why not?" Fritz glares at them. "Besides, it'll add a little buzz."

"Why do we need buzz?" Dick asks, glancing at James.

Storm is regaling a group of shirtless, red-trunked, Rehoboth Beach lifeguards with stories of his exploits during Superstorm Sandy when the trio arrives at the van.

"Storm," Fritz interrupts, "here are the gentle-men I wanted you to meet." He gives the lifeguards a withering look, and they reluctantly disperse.

"So pleased to meet you, Storm." James gives the weather reporter a strong handshake. "I'm a big fan."

"James used to play minor league baseball in the Yankees' system," Fritz says.

"Pitcher or catcher?" Storm says with a wink, giving James a not-so-subtle appraisal.

"First base," James replies, masterfully extracting his hand from yet another too-long handshake.

"Dick here writes historical biographies," Fritz continues. "He's hosting the hurricane party I told you about." The two men quickly shake hands.

"No disrespect, fellas, but I feel it's my duty," Storm's voice takes a serious tone, "as a weather professional to try and dissuade you from such an irresponsible activity. This storm is nothing to play around with. The state is taking this hurricane very seriously and is moving in its emergency ops team. I expect the governor will soon order an evacuation, and I'm certain the power company will shut off the grid to prevent the volatile mixture of sea-water and electricity from exploding into a wind-swept fireball."

One could see why his TV ratings were so high.

"That's all fine and dandy, but we're simply not

leaving," Fritz says. "I can't imagine where I would even evacuate to. Some cheap hotel in Dover? A local high school gymnasium? I don't think so."

"James here will have us well-prepared," Dick adds.

"Is that so?" says Storm.

"It's true," James says. "I follow the hurricane preparedness guide to a T."

Storm drapes his arm over James's shoulders. "Thank goodness someone here is taking this seriously." He leans in and whispers to James, "What's the address of this party?"

THE RAIN SQUALLS ARE BECOMING MORE FREQUENT, and large trees are waving about as if they are wispy palms. The cloud ceiling is dropping. Hurricane Chester is now about twelve hours away.

At Hunter House, James can hear the roar of waves crashing loudly onto the beach as he puts the cars in the garage and makes a last check around the cottage to remove any small items that might become hazardous projectiles in the hundred-mile-an-hour winds that are predicted to hit when the hurricane makes landfall.

Inside, he covers all the first-floor windows

and French doors with blankets and bedspreads to block out any signs of light and life, should any nosy police officers mosey down Pine Cone Lane looking for evacuation evaders. He sets up candles and hurricane lamps and charges all the cellphones and computers.

The usual crowd coming to Hunter House will be defying the governor's evacuation order for residents and visitors along the Delaware Coast—all seventeen miles of it. Henceforward, they must travel surreptitiously, so as not to attract attention.

Lil and Helen are the first to arrive. They'd moved their boat inland and had a hell of a time getting back to the coast, given that most of the main highways were evacuation routes going west. Fritz was right behind them, looking quite festive in a faded, tan-and-white seersucker suit. Kissy showed up attired in a yellow Helly Henson slicker she'd purchased just for the occasion. She'd been wearing a lot of yellow this year. It goes well, she tells everyone, with her strawberry-blonde hair and gold jewelry. Tagging along with her are Chip and Ashley Holzstock, who are riding out their first hurricane in Rehoboth.

"We brought a little hurricane gift," Ashley says, and presents a small, black box to Dick.

He lifts the lid to peek inside. "Cocktail napkins; how nice. We can always use these around Hunter House."

"Look closely." Ashley points, encouraging Dick to examine her gift.

Dick looks at the black toile pattern and to his great surprise sees not Frenchmen with powdered wigs, but Tom of Finland leather men with biker hats and bulging crotches.

"Dontcha just love it," screams Ashley. "Our gay friends Barry and Derek in New York just decorated their bedroom with that fabric."

"I even picked up a pair of boxer shorts in the same print," adds Chip. "Of course, I don't wear them on my gym day; don't wanna set off anyone's gaydar," Chip says with a wink.

"Come, let me pour you something to drink and show you Dick's wine closet," Kissy says, steering Ashley and Chip toward the kitchen. "I definitely think you should consider doing something similar in your remodel."

Dick is left standing in the entranceway, flabbergasted by this exchange, when Fritz approaches.

"Such tender scallops," Fritz purrs.

"I think he's wearing Tom of Finland underwear."

"I'm going to need a peek."

Before Fritz can leave, there's a knock on the door. Then another.

"Are you expecting anyone else?" Fritz whispers. The knocking becomes more insistent.

James comes into the hallway. "You don't think

it's the police?"

"Hello," a male voice yells. "Anyone home? It's Storm Chaser. I understand there's a party. Any chance a wet weatherman can find shelter and get a bite to eat on such a stormy night?"

Dick quickly opens the front door to reveal Storm, in his customary tight shorts and blue Weather Channel raincoat, holding a blown-out umbrella. He shakes like a dog and then enters.

"Why aren't you covering the storm, risking life and limb, to keep everyone informed?" Fritz asks.

"I have a precise three-hour break while America eats dinner. I go back on the air at primetime."

The party guests barrage Storm with questions about the hurricane, but before he can answer, there's a crack and a loud thud. Then another. Tree branches are dropping like pinecones. The lights flicker and then go out. Darkness envelops Hunter House. Rain hammers against the windows. Ashley Holzstock screams.

"Nothing to worry about," Storm announces. "We knew the power company was going to shut everything off for safety reasons."

The crowd breathes a collective sigh of relief as James lights the candles and hurricane lamps.

Lil opens her large purse and withdraws several folding camp-lanterns, a crank radio, waterproof matches, a small first-aid box, and a sewing kit. "Not to worry; I was a girl scout."

Once Storm is introduced, everyone settles in around a makeshift bar set up in the kitchen. James and Lil wander out onto the screened porch where they see Dick and Fritz, huddled outside under an orange and blue umbrella, trying to light a stack of charcoal briquettes on the old, black, Weber grill. Dick doesn't believe in gas grills or fireplaces.

"Think the rain might be coming down too hard?" James yells to the two men.

"Maybe," Fritz replies, rivulets of water running down his face.

"I think I've got an emergency poncho in here somewhere," says Lil, rooting around in her purse.

"I was sure the umbrella would work," Dick says. "Hey, what if we grill on the screened porch?"

"Too dangerous," James replies. "And what if the cops smell the smoke? We need to keep everything hush-hush."

"Well, gentlemen, we appear to be in a pickle." Dick looks at the wet grill.

Everyone in the grocery store had been purchasing canned goods and snack foods. Dick could not, in good faith, serve his guests baked beans and tuna fish, so he thought it would be nice to grill steaks and corn for dinner. The grocery store was practically giving away New York strips.

In the midst of a squall, the faint sound of a Frank Sinatra tune can be heard, along with a bicycle bell. Moments later, around the corner of the house appears a red, four-wheeled surrey with a red-and-white striped awning flapping wildly. It's big Dom, looking very much like a circus bear.

Dick escorts him inside; he is dripping wet and juggling two beautiful platters. Dom pulls off the plastic cover, revealing stacks of roasted yellow and red peppers, shaved prosciutto, fresh chunks of cantaloupe, grapes, olives, sweet pickles, pepperoni, salami, a wheel of creamy brie, and toasted almonds.

Dick looks at James questioningly.

"Hope you don't mind," James explains, "but I invited Dom over. He was having a hard time getting everything to fit into his coolers. I thought we could help him out by eating some of the inventory."

"A stellar idea, James!" Fitz exclaims. "My mouth is already watering for a bite of salami."

"Well done, James," Dick says. "I have a half-dozen bottles of that Italian Sangiovese we like. It will pair perfectly with antipasto."

As the guests gather around the platters of food, James begins opening bottles of wine. He feels something in his back pocket: a business card. Someone must have slipped it in while the power was out. He glances at it quickly, then drops it into the trashcan. "Who needs wine?" he asks.

All of a sudden, the music from the Weather Channel's "Local on the Eights" TV program starts playing.

"Where's my phone?" Storm yells, madly checking his numerous pockets. Everyone begins scrambling around, looking for the misplaced device.

"Got it," James says, handing it to Storm. "It was on the platter with the prosciutto."

Storm looks at his phone. "You're never gonna believe it … I've … I've never seen anything like it. Hurricane Chester has done a loop-de-loop and is now headed north to Long Island. The computer models now predict a landfall in the Hamptons."

The group in Dick's kitchen cheers.

"This means, dear friends, that I must depart immediately because, where the storm goes—"

"Storm goes," the crowd chants in unison.

"Correct," he replies. "I'm off to the Hamptons. But don't forget to follow me on Twitter."

And so, the charismatic weatherman departs in the same dramatic fashion as he arrived. The crowd in the kitchen begins to whoop it up.

Dick pulls James aside. "Though we were fortunate to escape a direct hit, you made sure we were ready for the worst. I appreciate that."

"Good preparation, my coach always told me, is the mother of luck."

"How lucky do you think we'll be to get this crowd out of here before midnight?" Dick gestures toward Fritz, who is taking out the Trivial Pursuit board game.

"Coach also said anything is possible. But by

the looks of things, I think the best we can hope for is that Fritz lands on the 'Sports' category often enough that he loses interest. I'm afraid the better advice for this situation might be: if you can't beat 'em, join 'em."

Noblesse Oblige

*Dick receives a jury summons, but
is he the one being judged?*

DICK AND JAMES ARE SIPPING COCKTAILS and admiring the moon rising over the ocean from the veranda of A. A. du Pont's large, shingle-style home on Queen Street. The occasion is A. A.'s annual autumn cocktail party, which is always held the night before the Rehoboth Beach Jazz Festival kicks off. The well-heeled crowd of two hundred is noshing and tippling, while chanteuse Holly Barry is pouring drinks and enchanting the crowd with a selection of jazz standards.

"I always wondered why your family didn't build a house right on the beach." James stretches his arms.

"My grandfather was a very particular man. He thought it was vulgar."

"A great view and the smell of sea air?"

Dick shrugs. "It was a different era. He believed a house at the beach should be shaded from the sun."

They cease their conversation upon the arrival of none other than Red Snapper, who is loudly guffawing, likely at one of his own corny jokes. A young man wearing a Royal Stewart tartan sport coat accompanies him. Despite the fact that the veranda is large, Red Snapper and his guest make a beeline for Dick and James.

"I thought you said this was the crème de la crème of Rehoboth society," James whispers as the two men approach.

"Gents, may I introduce you to Connor Luhgree. Mr. Luhgree is a lawyer from Charleston, South Carolina."

The men shake hands.

"A festive party," Connor says. The men all murmur their assent. "Very festive," he repeats. "Especially the singing bartender. You'd never see that in Charleston." He looks as if he has tasted something sour.

"What brings you to Rehoboth?" Dick asks, wondering why an attractive and apparently intelligent young man is on the arm of such an unrefined reprobate as Red Snapper.

"Visiting friends who own a home here."

"Who?" Dick asks. "Perhaps we know them? Do they —"

"I'm sure you don't," Red Snapper interrupts. "They're from Washington and certainly too young for you and your crowd."

"On that note, I think I'll go get us some more drinks." James excuses himself from the conversation and leaves Dick to deal with Red and Connor.

"So, Connor, what kind of law do you practice?"

"Trusts and estates and such."

"The Luhgree family is one of the most prestigious in Charleston," says Red Snapper with an exaggerated southern accent, to which Connor nods in solemn agreement.

"I wonder if you might share some advice," Dick begins. "I've received a summons for jury duty—"

"And like all good Americans, you want to find a way out," Red Snapper interrupts again.

"Inform them you have a law degree or that you distrust the local police force," Connor replies. "That's what I advise all my friends. Works like a charm."

"Actually, I was going to ask how to get selected. I want to serve."

Red Snapper's high, cold cackle pierces the air. "Why in hell would you want to waste your time in a Sussex County courtroom listening to tales of chicken-house arsons and trailer-park perversions?"

Dick didn't want to reveal that he'd always wanted to be on a jury, just like he'd always hoped to be part of an election-day exit poll. He thought he'd make an excellent juror, perhaps even a foreman. He was a voracious reader, after all, and that, he believed, rendered him extremely capable of projecting himself into the lives of others—even lives that have nothing in common with his own. As he begins to explain his position, Red Snapper snorts.

"It's called *empathy*, something you wouldn't understand." Dick looks directly at Red Snapper. "And, most importantly, I feel it's my civic duty."

"Ah yes," Red Snapper replies, his jaw tight. "*Noblesse oblige*. How quaint. Dick's family made their fortune selling toenail clippers."

"Paper clips," Dick rebuts.

"Hmmm." Connor looks unimpressed.

James reappears with two fresh cocktails just as Red Snapper and Connor are starting to pull away.

"Always nice to see you, James," Red Snapper says with a leer and a squeeze to James's bicep. "And say hello to that charming sister of yours," he says to Dick. "She's a patient of mine," he explains to Connor, while guiding him back toward the French doors and the party inside.

James brushes off his arm in an exaggerated manner. "What was that show and tell all about?"

"His usual antics." Dick watches the pair depart. "At first I felt sorry for Mr. Connor Luhgree, but now I get the sense that they're two peas in a pod."

JAMES IS LIGHTLY SCRAMBLING EGGS in brown butter, the way Julia Child recommended, when Dick enters the kitchen.

"What do you think of my Dominick Dunne ensemble," he asks, doing a slow turnaround to model his horn-rim glasses, purple-checked shirt, and pressed chinos.

"I'm not following." James wags a spatula up and down at Dick. "This is how you normally dress. And who is Dominick Dunne?"

Ah, sweet youth, Dick thinks. "The late Dominick Dunne was a *Vanity Fair* writer who specialized in celebrity court cases."

"So why are you channeling a dead writer, and what does it have to do with jury duty?"

"Everything," Dick says, as he sits at the table. James joins him, bringing two plates of steaming eggs.

What Dick had learned in his preparatory research is that while much has been written about how to *avoid* jury service, there is very little information about how to *get selected.*

"The experts on the art and science of jury selection report that lawyers tend to favor jurors who are well-groomed and well-dressed, but not flashy. And it's important to look interested."

"Go on," James says, between mouthfuls.

"You probably don't remember it, but Dominick Dunne actually came to Sussex County in 2005 to cover the big Disney lawsuit over one of Michael Eisner's sweetheart deals."

"You should eat before it gets cold," James says, pointing at Dick's plate.

"In a minute. You know, I had the good fortune to meet Dominick Dunne. It was at the most delightful little dinner party."

"Go on."

"From what I recall, our Delaware lawyers and judges seemed to like him. So to raise my chances of getting selected, I've decided to impersonate the late Mr. Dunne."

"Well, it can't hurt," James replies, with only a small degree of skepticism.

"Precisely. With any luck, by day's end, I shall be a juror."

"Hmmm," James watches as Dick tucks a napkin into his collar and finally starts on his eggs.

A SKINNY WOMAN SMOKING A CIGARETTE and lugging a plastic, red-and-white Igloo cooler gets in line behind Dick as he waits outside the courthouse for the doors to open.

"Brought me some ham samiches and a couple cans of Dr. Pepper," she tells Dick.

"I don't think you're allowed to bring in food."

"I'm gonna tell them boys," she gestures toward the officials now starting to let people into the building, "that my medicines need to stay cool."

We'll see how that goes. Dick smiles politely. Per court instructions, he'd left behind all electronic devices, newspapers, and magazines. He only carries with him a first edition of Hillary Clinton's book *Hard Choices* so the lawyers will see he is a serious man who is familiar with difficult decision-making.

He follows the queue through security into the courthouse, then up a set of stairs and down a long hallway into a large courtroom. Portraits of important-looking judges hang on the walls. Dick takes a seat on the uncomfortable wooden bench and scopes out his rivals: a fat, sweaty man in a tight, navy-blue suit; a young hipster with Elvis-sized sideburns; and an older woman with big, pink rollers in her hair. He can't help but feel confident about his chances of being picked.

After a short informational video, the court clerk begins calling names for the day's prospective jury pool. Dick's name is announced first. They might claim it's random selection, he thinks, but clearly, his careful preparations have paid off. He struts past rows of his peers, making sure to flash the lawyers a glimpse of *Hard Choices.*

The jury pool is escorted downstairs and into a windowless holding room with a big, flat-screen television mounted to a wall. There's an air of excitement that soon deflates when the court clerk comes in and turns on the television to *Wheel of Fortune*.

"Personally," Dick says to the woman whose cooler had been confiscated, "I would show old reruns of *Perry Mason*." She coughs.

Dick notices the prospective jurors beginning to spread out and self-select into interest groups. Cooler Lady joins the "talkers" on the right side of the room. "Watchers" move in front of the television, while "sleepers" go to the farthest corner of the room. Dick joins the "readers" in the middle of the room, but soon tires of Hillary Clinton's pontificating about the transatlantic rifts that opened up during the Bush administration, so he begins to eavesdrop on the "talkers."

Over the next two hours, he learns that goats are better than cows and sheep at pasture maintenance, and that Aruba is best avoided as a vacation destination if you're a blonde because "they'll kill you." He hears someone say that nobody believes the reality show "Married at First Sight," but then Cooler Lady — between coughing fits — claims it happened to her. Seems she sobered up for the first time in weeks on her wedding day. That was her second wedding, though, so it didn't really count.

When three burly policemen escort two prisoners in handcuffs and jumpsuits right by the open door of the room, everyone gets excited. Was this it? Were those the men they'd see at trial? The court clerk returns shortly to call the panelists to voir dire, which Dick knows from his research is the interview process through which the lawyers select a jury panel.

Dick and his peers file back into the courtroom where they had started. A lawyer explains the process and summarizes the criminal case: A fight between two women—one a Washington Redskins fan and the other a Philadelphia Eagles fan—broke out over a disputed Redskins touchdown call during a Sunday afternoon football game on the big screen at the Tuna Tower Bar. It escalated into a drunken car chase, which ended up with both women driving onto the beach and getting their vehicles stuck in the sand, whereupon the Eagles fan dragged the Redskins fan by her hair down to the surf and tried to drown her. The cops intervened, and luckily, no one was seriously hurt.

"I know them girls!" yells the Cooler Lady, who is immediately dismissed, along with a couple of other prospective jurors who claim to either patronize the Tuna Tower on a regular basis, or feel the Redskins fan got what she deserved.

Dick is both mortified and excited. All these dismissals before individual questioning even begins seems to tip the scales in his favor. On the other hand, he knows very little about pro football or female wrestling.

Dick is finally called to appear in front of the

lawyers. His questioning appears to be going well until the defense attorney asks about the book Dick is not so subtly displaying.

"It's Hillary Clinton's book. I wanted you to see that I, too, am smart and extremely capable of making the tough choices required of a juror." Dick points out the title of the book to the lawyers. "Some others here are reading books, too, but you'll notice they're just cheap paperbacks with metallic, embossed titles."

As Dick begins to explain how he is channeling the late author Dominick Dunne, the defense attorney puts forth a peremptory challenge and, just like that, Dick Hunter is dismissed.

"What? But I'd be the perfect juror," Dick exclaims, standing his ground. "Ask me some more questions. Give me another chance. At least tell me what I did wrong."

The clerk of the court escorts Dick out of the courtroom and into the hallway, where he explains that a peremptory challenge doesn't require the lawyer to give a reason. "Sir, the bottom line is that the court will not require your services today."

"But I've come all this way from Rehoboth. Isn't there another trial I could try out for? I came to do my civic duty, not to watch game shows."

"Call in later tonight for instructions," the clerk says. He turns and departs, leaving Dick standing dazed and alone outside the courtroom. Just

140

as Dick is about to re-enter the courtroom and ask again for a second chance, he hears his name called. He turns and is relieved to see James.

"I thought you might get a lunch break and, lo and behold, here you are."

"I've been dismissed for the day. I spent the entire morning just sitting around, waiting."

"I hear that often happens. Let's go grab some lunch. I have something that might cheer you up."

The men head out of the courthouse, which is situated on the town green—actually a large roundabout creating a quaint setting reminiscent of something you'd see in England.

"I think you're going to like the Downtown Restaurant," says James, pointing to the restaurant's sign as they cross the street.

"Clever name," Dick says.

"It's where Dominick Dunne had lunch every day while he was following the Disney trial," James explains. On his phone, he shows Dick a *Los Angeles Times* photo of Dunne eating soup in the very same restaurant.

Dick's face brightens immediately, and he excitedly pulls James into the restaurant. Looking at James's phone, Dick guides them to the booth in the photo.

"Just think. This is the exact place Dunne sat every day." He looks around. "I can't believe they haven't put up a plaque."

A waitress with a notepad comes over to take their order. "What can I get you guys?"

Dick asks her to please bring him what Dominick Dunne liked for lunch. She just looks at him, not saying a word. Dick grabs James's phone and shows her the photo of Dunne.

"Yeah. OK. What can I get you?"

Outside, it begins to rain.

"I believe you have some famous lima bean soup?" James inquires, eying an enormous sign above the takeout counter that says, "Try our famous lima bean soup."

"We'll each have a bowl, please," says Dick. "And two glasses of chardonnay."

"We don't serve wine. This is a family restaurant."

DICK NEVER DID GET SELECTED for a trial during the two weeks he was on call. In hindsight, he confessed to James that the Hillary Clinton book might have been too partisan and put them off. Next time, perhaps he'd be better served flaunting de Tocqueville or Ayn Rand.

In any case, he had to face the reality that his plan, while well-executed, had failed. He consoled himself with the fact that, although the experience was disappointing, he did find a good cup of homemade lima bean soup—in fact, the best he'd ever tasted. It was a favorite, he told everyone, of the late Dominick Dunne.

A Moment's Peace

Everyone needs Dick's help, when
all he wants is a nap.

AT PRECISELY THREE O'CLOCK post meridiem, Dick Hunter lies down on his king-sized bed for an afternoon nap.

Whenever he is engrossed in a writing project—as he is now with the biography of Henry Cogswell—Dick finds it easier to work when he knows he has his nap to look forward to after lunch. It simply makes each half of the day more enjoyable.

He places his eyeglasses on the bedside table and has just closed his eyes when the ear-splitting screams of a half-dozen leaf blowers start up simultaneously.

He looks out the bedroom window. Yep, he can see the full lawn brigade over at Red Snapper's place. He's certain his old nemesis has told them to use more blowers than they need, just to spite him.

He turns over, his back to the window, and tries to ignore the blowers. Just as he starts to drift off, his cellphone rings.

"Hello!" Dick barks.

"My, such a friendly greeting."

"I'm sorry, Fritz. It's just the damn leaf blowers at Red Snapper's are making a terrible racket, and I'm trying to take a nap."

"Call the police on him for a noise violation."

"I don't think that's going to work. What were you calling about, anyway?"

"Listen, I'll be brief. I need a short-term loan. Just a— Hello? Dick? Are you there?"

"Yes, I can hear you."

"You've been pestering me to fix the holes in my roof."

"For months now. It's disgraceful."

"Yes, well, uh, I just saw Storm Chaser on the Weather Channel predicting more Nor'easters this winter. By the way, I think he's dying his hair. It looks too blond. Anyway, he's convinced me it's time."

"You will listen to him but not to me?"

"Now don't get testy. He's a weather profession-al. You really ought to take that nap."

"I'm trying."

"The problem is my next quarterly trust pay-ment is months away, and it will be even smaller than the last one. I was looking around at some fur-niture to sell, but I'm afraid it will take too long to find a serious buyer. Could you provide me with a short-term loan? It would be a big help."

"Fine." Dick could never say no to a friend in need, and especially not to Fritz. "How much do you need? Twenty thousand?"

"Um—well, sure—for an asphalt roof. But I was thinking the right thing to do would be to replace the cedar shakes. An even better idea would be a combination of cedar shakes on the first and second floor levels and copper roofing for the porch roofs and gutters, like the Holzstock couple did with the old Reynolds cottage. That looks fabulous, but they tell me I'm looking at about fifty thousand."

Dick remains silent.

"Dick, can you hear me?"

"Loud and clear, despite the leaf blowers."

"You know I always pay back my loans."

"Of course. I'm sorry. I'm just aggravated. Drop by tomorrow, and I'll write you a check."

"That's—"

"I've got to go. The leaf blowers have stopped, so I can get back to my nap now. I'll talk to you later."

"OK. Knew I could count on you. Merci beaucoup!"

The secret to a good nap, Dick believes, is not to remove one's clothes and not to get under the covers—and always leave a light on. It's critically important to keep the distinction between taking a nap and going to bed. A good nap should come after lunch and before cocktail hour. And it should last no longer than ninety minutes.

Just as he adjusts the pillows correctly, he is startled by the sound of electronic air-kisses. It's a phone ring he knows all too well. It's also a ring he knows won't stop until he answers the call.

"Hello, Kissy," he says, in the cheeriest tone he can muster.

"Listen, I'm out with a client, and we're wondering if we can pop by for a second. I want to show her your kitchen and study."

"I'm taking a nap."

"How funny," says Kissy, "since you're talking to me."

"OK, I'm *trying* to take a nap."

"Dick Hunter, you have perfected the art of doing nothing."

"I beg your pardon?"

"Never mind. I promise, promise, promise we won't stay long. You won't even know we're there. Take your little nap, and I'll use my key so you don't even need to come downstairs and properly greet us."

"Your key?"

"Just never you mind. Go ahead and take your nap."

Naturally, the two women are anything but quiet. Dick scowls when he hears the unmistakable pop of a cork. *Good Lord, they're drinking my wine.*

He rolls over and wraps a pillow around his

head, but it's still not enough to drown out the conversation. Around four o'clock, he hears chairs clattering and the sound of a bottle being tossed into the recycling bin. The front door slams shut, and he hears the spewing of pea gravel as Kissy guns her BMW out of the driveway. Not more than a minute or two later, the doorbell rings.

What now, he wonders, peering out the bedroom window. *Damn.* It's his sister Jane, to whom he has barely spoken since the night she came to dinner. He hesitates before opening the window.

"Jane, up here."

His sister backs up and looks toward the voice, hand shielding her eyes from the afternoon sun. "What took you so long? I need your help."

"I'm trying to take a nap."

"Why?"

"Why not?"

"Mother always said you were lazy."

"I am not lazy. I am merely in tune with my circadian rhythms. And if you've come by just to insult me, I shall have to ask you to leave."

"It's about Little Nat."

"Nothing bad, I hope?"

"He's still in the clutches of that New York Jewess."

Dick grimaces. "You mean his fiancé."

"Please don't use that word; I can't bear it. Her father is moving full-steam ahead with the wedding and the reception in East Hampton."

"Isn't it traditional for the bride's family to select the venue for the wedding?"

"Yes, but that's why I'm here. We have an opportunity to influence that. May I come in?"

"I suppose."

"The door is locked."

"I'll be right down." Dick reluctantly gets out of bed and drags himself downstairs to open the front door.

Jane follows Dick into his study, and the siblings sit down to talk.

"You're looking rather disheveled this afternoon," Jane says, looking Dick up and down.

"Merely rumpled, dear sister. Tell me why you're here."

"Little Nat tells me his fiancé is worried about her family's financial situation," Jane starts off. "Not only is her father's second wife divorcing him, but her younger twin sisters just started at Brown. If we could offer to pay for the wedding, then we'd call the shots."

"Uh—"

"We could have it here at a proper Episcopal church and hold the reception at the family house, um, I mean your house."

"Why are you dragging me into this?"

"Little Nat is your godson. All I need you to do is pay. I'll handle the rest. You know things are still tough for me with Big Nat in jail. And you got all that money from Aunt Evelyn when she died. I didn't see a penny."

"Because she didn't like you," Dick says, gritting his teeth.

"I'm desperate, Dick. Please don't turn your back on your family in a time of crisis. We've got to stop this Hamptons wedding."

"OK, OK. I'll do it."

"You'll do what?" says James. Dick and Jane hadn't heard him come in.

"It's a long story." Dick looks at his watch—five o'clock. "And now it's too late for a nap," he says with a sigh. Too late for a nap, but fortunately, not too early for cocktails. "I think I'll have a French 75. Anyone else?"

"That would be nice, thank you," says Jane.

When Dick and James go to the kitchen, Jane sees the opportunity to make another attempt to take Dick's will. She quickly looks around.

"Where did he put that strongbox?" she mutters. She scans the contents of the room until she spies it, now on the bottom shelf of one of the bookcases.

Jane drops to her knees and tries to open the box. "Damn!" It's locked this time. James must have secured it after catching her with it last time. She puts it back just as her brother returns with a tray of cocktails and a small dish of goldfish crackers.

"Here we go." Dick hands her a flute. "Let's

drink a toast to the family, as dysfunctional as it—and your plan—may be."

"What plan?" Jane says nervously.

"Why the wedding plan, of course," Dick responds.

"Oh, of course." Jane squirms and glances quickly at James, whose face is a blank slate. She takes a swallow of her drink and sits back in the chair.

Jane's plan to steal the will has been foiled again. Is it her imagination, or is James enjoying her discomfort? Certainly the little gold digger isn't smart enough to have figured out her plan. For now, she is out of options, but damned if she'll give up. She gulps the cocktail, which goes down like a dry pill.

Auld Lang Syne

The year ends in a blaze of glory.

"SO YOU'RE TELLING US this fireplace is the sole source of heat in Fritz Wilmerding's entire house?"

Dick is fielding questions from the Kimonos, a gay couple known about town for gardening in kimonos and clogs. Dick could never remember their names.

"It's why he doesn't use a fireplace screen. Screens absorb and block heat," Dick explains while stepping on and rubbing out an ember that just popped out onto the old Persian rug. The taller Kimono watches Dick's foot put out the ember and then notices all the burn marks on the rug.

"Technically, he shouldn't even be using it," Dick says. "The last chimney sweep told Fritz it wasn't safe."

"Really?"

"Now he builds fires only for special occasions," Dick adds, while warming his hands over the crackling fire. "Why do you think the invitation for tonight's soiree specified cashmere sweaters or sport coats as a dress code?"

The Kimonos look at each other.

"This place was originally built as a three-season cottage, back when nobody stayed in Rehoboth during the winter. Fritz has neither heating nor air conditioning." Dick pauses for effect. "He also heats with light bulbs."

"No!"

"If you were to open those drawers," Dick points to a large, antique, mahogany chest on the far side of the living room, "you would find Fritz's cache of incandescent light bulbs. He hoards them because the new CFL bulbs don't give off nearly as much heat."

Dick laughs as the Kimonos scurry over to look in the chest.

"What are you up to?" James asks, sidling up to Dick. He is accompanied by Rehoboth's best-known purveyor of deli meats and cheese, Dom Orso, who is wearing a black, mink car coat.

"Just explaining to the Kimonos why it's so chilly in here."

"You don't have to tell me." Dom pulls up the collar of his coat. "It's a little ridiculous, don't you think? A simple space heater costs less than a hundred dollars."

"Now, Dom, you should know by now that Fritz is all about the performance. Practicality does not figure into it. I still remember that New Year's Eve when he tossed the Hitchcock chair into the fire after it collapsed under you."

"That chair was rickety to begin with!"

"Of course," Dick says. "As are all of Fritz's chairs. I hold my breath every time I sit down."

"Then there was the time," Dom begins, with a laugh, "when he got drunk and shoved his Christmas tree into the fireplace, decorations and all. Said he'd had enough of the holiday. I thought for sure he was going to burn down the house."

"It's all very *Doctor Zhivago*, and that's precisely why—" Dick is interrupted by the sound of a loud gong.

"Gentlemen," Fritz announces, before striking the gong again, "please take your assigned seats. Dinner is about to commence."

Fritz Wilmerding is extremely proud of his formal dining room. It sets him apart, he believes, from the newcomers and their contemporary floor plans and dining areas with phony wainscoting. It's so much nicer, he always says, when you can have your guests seated in a formal dining room and make an entrance with the food.

Dick and James, Dom, and the Kimonos circle the large, highly polished, mahogany dining-room table in search of their names on the place cards. A Wagner opera is playing, and one would be hard-pressed to tell if the pops and crackles are coming from the fireplace or the old vinyl recording.

Couples are split, which means Dick is seated next to the shorter Kimono. It is a simple gathering—but a coveted invitation—for New Year's Eve dinner is one of the very few times Fritz entertains anymore.

But when he does entertain, Fritz pulls out all the stops. Dick has to give him credit. A pair of ornate, brass, five-arm candelabras featuring fifteen-inch, red, tapered candles anchor the table setting—and distract from the ceiling warped by water damage. The best Wilmerding family plates and silverware are on display. There are water glasses, white-wine glasses, red-wine glasses, and champagne flutes. My God, he'd even polished up his silver napkin rings.

This was the Kimonos' first visit to Fritz's house, and Dick watched his dinner companions' eyes roam across the table tableau to the Wilmerding family portraits gracing the paint-peeled walls. Large, silver champagne buckets and ceramic vases filled with magnolia and holly sprays are tucked here and there in odd places.

"What's with all the buckets and vases?" the shorter Kimono asks Dick.

"Because it's raining. Look closely, and I think you'll see they function as cisterns to catch water dripping from the ceiling. Fritz has holes in his roof," Dick whispers. "One is the size of a basketball. He was supposed to have it repaired, but then stated he wouldn't have a construction project ruining the ambience of his New Year's Eve party."

"You're kidding."

"Watch closely." The shorter Kimono follows Dick's advice and, lo and behold, soon witnesses several drips landing in a vase.

The men's conversation is interrupted when Fritz brings out a platter of roasted oysters, collected yesterday, he tells everyone, from the Chesapeake Bay. The bivalves are followed by the main course—a rack of lamb with rosemary and thyme, accompanied by whipped white potatoes and haricots verts. It is a traditional French fête, for sure. Few people knew of Fritz's culinary prowess.

For dessert, Fritz presents a yule log sponge cake with coffee buttercream and chocolate ganache.

"I'll have you know, it's sprinkled with edible gold dust, and the white mushrooms sprouting from the log and the plate it's on are made from meringue."

"Now this is truly perverse," Dick says softly, as the guests all applaud the dramatic dessert. "Mushrooms to accompany the mildew."

"What do you mean?" asks the shorter Kimono.

"Mildew is everywhere," Dick says, while gesturing about the dining room, "only you can't see it in the dim lighting he keeps."

Meanwhile, the sound of water dripping into the vases is getting louder as the rainstorm intensifies. But, of course, everyone at the table ignores it, especially because Fritz has reappeared from the kitchen holding a huge, leather book, on top of which is a silver tray containing liquor bottles and colorful, round, drinking glasses.

"No Wilmerding party is complete without a surprise," Dick announces to the dinner guests.

Fritz carefully slides the drink tray onto a small buffet in front of the row of windows overlooking what once was a formal, boxwood garden but is now a giant tangle of runaway English ivy. He brings the leather book with him and gently places it on the dining table.

"Voila!" Fritz is beaming. "It's all here, gentlemen." He pats the book.

Waiting for a reaction and getting none, he continues: "For the past year, I've been writing my memoirs, a fantastic tell-all about our gay beau monde here in Rehoboth. Tales of the city, handwritten with love. And in case you're wondering—yes—you all make an appearance!" Fritz claps. His guests remain silent.

Fritz turns to Dom. "Remember the hustlers at your first restaurant? Those in the know," he explains to his guests, "could ask for Dom's special 'beef menu.' It had the names, descriptions, predilections, and phone numbers for rent boys who'd come down from Philly to work in Rehoboth on summer weekends."

Dom shrugs his shoulders. "Had to pay the bills somehow — "

Fritz looks to Dick. "Remember when that crazy Greek boyfriend of yours kidnapped your mother?"

"He did not kidnap her."

"He locked her in the trunk of her own Cadillac and drove around town for four hours drinking ouzo until you agreed to buy him some gaudy sapphire ring he'd had his eye on. I'd say that qualifies as kidnapping."

"She wasn't in the trunk," Dick explains. "She was in the back seat, and Hermes was controlling the locks from the driver's seat."

Fritz turns to the Kimonos. "And of course, I haven't forgotten about the wild, after-hours, hot-tub parties you two used to host with all those closeted Republicans from DC. Oh, those were the days!"

Noticing the uncomfortable looks on the faces of the men around the table, James pipes up. "But why dredge up these stories? Do you really want to alienate your friends?"

"Moi? Of course not. These are merely funny little vignettes that readers will love. Besides, I've changed the names. For example, I refer to Dick as Nick. Dom is Don. And I never use last names."

"Truman Capote did the exact same thing," Dick says. "He exposed his friends' secrets. It ruined all his important relationships and some say his career, too."

"Don't be such a party pooper. It will be fabulous. And to celebrate, I'm going to make us some Bailey's comets."

Fritz scurries over to the buffet and begins mixing up the alcoholic concoction. He floats a layer of 151-proof rum on top of each drink and then sets the high-octane liquor on fire, while sprinkling cinnamon, which sparkles like a comet's tail. He looks extraordinarily pleased with himself.

Once everyone has a flaming drink in hand, Fritz raises a glass in toast: "To a new year and to good friends. Chin-Chin!"

At that moment, the glasses begin to explode, one by one. Apparently, Fritz's antique glassware wasn't designed to handle flaming drinks.

Glass particles and flaming liquid shower everyone and everything. Dick's camel cashmere jacket looks like a Pollack painting. As the guests recoil, one of the candelabras is knocked over, igniting a couple of the paper place cards and the old, dry tablecloth.

The flames grow quickly, fanned by the draft blowing across the dining room from the windows, which aren't insulated and don't close properly. The remaining meringue mushrooms begin to char, atop what is now an actual smoldering yule log.

During the ruckus and the rush of dinner guests exiting the dining room, James surreptitiously pushes the open leather book toward the flames. The pages catch fire quickly.

Fritz returns with a rusty, red fire extinguisher and attempts to put out the fire, but of course, the old extinguisher is empty. Seeing his manuscript in flames, he screams, and then grabs one of the big flower vases on the floor and empties its water onto the leather book. But by that time, most of the pages have burned.

"My memoirs!" Fritz cries, and slumps into a chair, which collapses beneath him.

DRIVING HOME IN THE METROPOLITAN later that night, Dick and James are recounting the evening's debacle. "I've seen a lot of odd things on New Year's Eve at Fritz's," Dick says with a laugh, "but the table fire has to take the cake, so to speak."

"I can't believe he wrote his memoirs by hand instead of using a computer," James replies, "so he had no backup."

"A year's work, gone up in flames, literally. What's the chance of that happening?" Dick wonders aloud.

After a moment's delay, James speaks. "Fire is funny. It leaps and moves as if it has a life of its own."

"I guess you're right."

"But in the end, it does seem like a fortunate

outcome."

"I wholeheartedly agree."

"It was a strangely fitting end to a pretty good year overall, don't you think?"

"Thanks to you. I don't know what I'd do without you."

"Well, you know what they say, right?" asks James.

"All's well that ends well?" says Dick.

"And tomorrow is another day."

The Drink Recipes

Dick's Unflagging Delight
The French 75

Ingredients

- 2 ounces dry gin, preferably Plymouth
- ¼ ounce Grand Marnier, preferably Quintessence
- Juice of half a Meyer lemon
- Champagne

Directions

Pour gin, Grand Marnier, and lemon juice in a cocktail shaker. Fill with ice and shake vigorously. Strain into an iced flute and fill with champagne. Stir gently. Garnish with a lemon twist.

This cocktail looks deceptively simple but packs a powerful punch. It was named after a mobile cannon used in World War I. A smooth, refreshing mix, it is Dick's go-to cocktail for a sophisticated dinner party, a celebration, or even a round of cocktail croquet. The secret to Dick's version of the French 75 is the substitution of the Meyer lemon for the everyday lemon and the use of a very special Grand Marnier—Quintessence. Quintessence is made with much older cognacs and uses a double parfum process in which orange peels are distilled twice. It costs about $800 a bottle, but it's well worth it if you can find it. One other thing—Dick isn't a stickler for a flute; a highball glass works just fine.

James's Juicy Juice
Sangria

Ingredients

- 2 bottles of chilled dry red wine, preferably Rioja
- 1 cup of brandy
- 1 cup of orange juice
- 1/4 cup of superfine granulated sugar
- 2 teaspoons guava jelly
- 2 oranges, cut into thin rounds
- 2 lemons, cut into thin rounds
- 3 limes, cut into thin rounds
- 2 apples, cored and cut into 1/2-inch chunks
- 2 cups of cold club soda

Directions

In a large pot or bowl, mix the sugar, guava jelly, and orange juice until the sugar and jelly dissolve. Pour in the wine and brandy and stir until everything is blended. Add the orange, lemon, lime slices, and apples. Refrigerate until well chilled — at least one hour if you're in a hurry. James lets his sit overnight to better blend the flavors. Remove from the refrigerator and add the club soda. Serve in glasses over ice.

Sangria is an unpretentious, refreshing, and easy-to-make summer cocktail that is perfect for a day on the beach or an evening on the screened porch. Most recipes suggest using any old wine you have around the house. James prefers a drier red wine, a dab of guava jelly, and he'll slip in a few peaches when they're in season.

Flamboyantly Fritz
The Bailey's Comet

Ingredients

- 1 ½ ounces Bailey's Irish Cream
- 1 ½ ounces butterscotch Schnapps
- ¾ ounce Goldschläger
- 1/2 ounce 151-proof rum
- 1 dash cinnamon

Directions

Pour the Bailey's, Schnapps, and Goldschlager into a cocktail shaker. Fill with ice and shake vigorously. Strain into a cocktail glass. Add a shallow layer of 151-proof rum on top. Light the rum on fire, then immediately sprinkle a generous dash of cinnamon on top while serving. The cinnamon will sparkle like a comet's tail.

This flaming cocktail is a production number, so of course, Fritz Wilmerding would want to serve it for a special occasion. He also knows it's easier to make than it looks, and it tastes better than it sounds. It's the perfect drinkable dessert. Plus, if he ups the amount of 151-proof rum, he'll up the flame. Bigger is always better, in Fritz's opinion, although he recommends not using antique glassware.

A Kissy Cocktail
The Manhattan, Ordered Up

Ingredients

- 3 ounces bourbon whiskey
- 3 drops Italian sweet Vermouth
- Garnish with one wild Italian candied cherry

Directions

Pour whiskey and drops of Vermouth in a mixing glass with cracked ice. Gently stir and strain. Pour into a pre-chilled, V-style, stemmed cocktail glass. Garnish.

There isn't one correct way to make a Manhattan, and that makes it the quintessentially American cocktail. As a Southern woman, Kissy makes hers with good Kentucky bourbon. And though she prefers her Manhattan "up," she's not averse to simply pouring some bourbon and Vermouth into a glass, adding ice, and stirring with her pinky finger. Heck, sometimes she even forgoes the Vermouth, but she never forgoes the cherry.

Jane's Morning Medicine
Bloody Mary

Ingredients

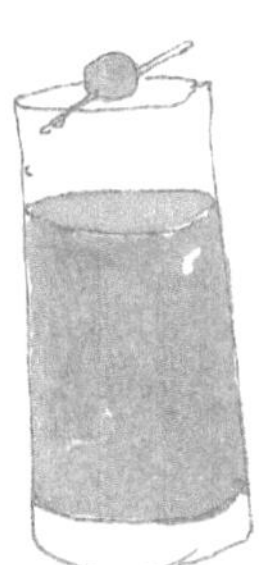

- 4 ounces Clamato juice
- 5 drops Tabasco sauce
- 5 squirts of a lime
- 3 ounces vodka
- Twist of a pepper mill
- Cocktail olives

Directions

A perfect bloody mary, according to Jane, should be light and not clogged with debris. One should strive to achieve a harmony between the Clamato juice and the vodka. And whatever you do, avoid the ubiquitous celery stick — it just takes up volume that would be better devoted to vodka.

Take any glass and add 4 ounces of Clamato juice. Follow with five dashes of Tabasco sauce — the classic flavor, not the nouveau jalapeño, chipotle, or habanero versions, and five squirts from a real lime. Add 3 ounces of vodka, a twist of fresh pepper, and garnish with an olive. Sip repeatedly.

What's next for Dick and James?

Will Jane be able to cut James out of the will?

Will Red Snapper finally get the best of Dick?

How long will Fritz's roof hold out?

And what will the Pie Ladies do next?

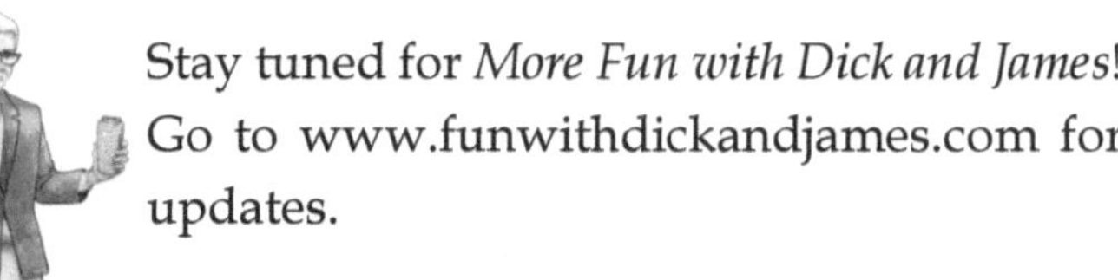

Stay tuned for *More Fun with Dick and James*!
Go to www.funwithdickandjames.com for
updates.

Want more adventures for Dick and James?
Help us out by posting a review
on Amazon or Goodreads.